THE RIME OF THE ANCIENT MARINER AND OTHER POEMS

Samuel Taylor Coleridge

COLLINS
CLASSICS

William Collins
An imprint of HarperCollins*Publishers*
1 London Bridge Street
London SE1 9GF

WilliamCollinsBooks.com

This William Collins paperback edition
published in Great Britain in 2016

3

A catalogue record for this book
is available from the British Library

ISBN 978-0-00-816756-1

Printed and bound by
CPI Group (UK) Ltd, Croydon, CR0 4YY

MIX
Paper from
responsible sources
FSC C007454

FSC™ is a non-profit international organisation established to promote the responsible management of the world's forests. Products carrying the FSC label are independently certified to assure consumers that they come from forests that are managed to meet the social, economic and ecological needs of present and future generations, and other controlled sources.

Find out more about HarperCollins and the environment at
www.harpercollins.co.uk/green

Classic Literature: Words and Phrases adapted from
Collins English Dictionary

Typesetting in Kalix by Palimpsest Book Production Limited,
Falkirk, Stirlingshire

History of William Collins

In 1819, millworker William Collins from Glasgow, Scotland, set up a company for printing and publishing pamphlets, sermons, hymn books and prayer books. That company was Collins and was to mark the birth of HarperCollins Publishers as we know it today. The long tradition of Collins dictionary publishing can be traced back to the first dictionary William published in 1824, *Greek and English Lexicon*. Indeed, from 1840 onwards, he began to produce illustrated dictionaries and even obtained a licence to print and publish the Bible.

Soon after, William published the first Collins novel, *Ready Reckoner*; however, it was the time of the Long Depression, where harvests were poor, prices were high, potato crops had failed and violence was erupting in Europe. As a result, many factories across the country were forced to close down and William chose to retire in 1846, partly due to the hardships he was facing.

Aged 30, William's son, William II, took over the business. A keen humanitarian with a warm heart and a generous spirit, William II was truly 'Victorian' in his outlook. He introduced new, up-to-date steam presses and published affordable editions of Shakespeare's works and *The Pilgrim's Progress*, making them available to the masses for the first time. A new demand for educational books meant that success came with the publication of travel books, scientific books, encyclopedias and dictionaries. This demand to be educated led to the later publication of atlases, and Collins also held the monopoly on scripture writing at the time.

In the 1860s Collins began to expand and diversify

and the idea of 'books for the millions' was developed. Affordable editions of classical literature were published, and in 1903 Collins introduced 10 titles in their Collins Handy Illustrated Pocket Novels. These proved so popular that a few years later this had increased to an output of 50 volumes, selling nearly half a million in their year of publication. In the same year, The Everyman's Library was also instituted, with the idea of publishing an affordable library of the most important classical works, biographies, religious and philosophical treatments, plays, poems, travel and adventure. This series eclipsed all competition at the time, and the introduction of paperback books in the 1950s helped to open that market and marked a high point in the industry.

HarperCollins is and has always been a champion of the classics, and the current Collins Classics series follows in this tradition – publishing classical literature that is affordable and available to all. Beautifully packaged, highly collectible and intended to be reread and enjoyed at every opportunity.

Life & Times

About the Author

Samuel Taylor Coleridge was an English poet, philosopher and critic. A great friend of William Wordsworth, he was a founder of the Romantic movement in English literature, and is regarded as one of the most important poets of the period. He died at the age of 61, having battled lifelong ill health and an opium addiction.

Early Years

Coleridge was born in 1772 in Devon, the youngest of thirteen children of the Reverend John Coleridge, a vicar and headmaster. The reverend died when Samuel was just eight, and he was dispatched to London to attend Christ's Hospital. There, under the tutelage of a stern but inspirational schoolmaster, he was introduced to the Greek and Roman poets as well as Shakespeare and Milton.

Musing on his school days in 1817's *Biographia Literaria; or Biographical Sketches of My Literary Life and Opinions*, Coleridge recalls how the Reverend James Bowyer drilled into him that 'poetry, even that of the loftiest and, seemingly, that of the wildest odes, had a logic of its own, as severe as that of science; and more difficult, because more subtle, more complex'. Bowyer's approach to poetic composition was no-nonsense in the extreme, but it instilled in Coleridge a sensitivity to syntax and imagery, and sent him off to Cambridge University full of 'good gifts'. He proved a more enthusiastic poet than student, however, accumulating large debts and a collection of juvenile poems but never completing his degree.

Idealists and Romantics

Coleridge's education did at least serve to throw him into the company of young men who would later form his literary circle. At Christ's Hospital he befriended Charles Lamb, and as a student he met Robert Southey, a fellow poet and idealist with whom he hatched a plan to found a commune in the wilds of America, where learning and liberty would reign supreme. In 1795 the two young men married sisters Edith and Sarah Fricker – Southey happily, Coleridge very unhappily – and plans for the commune eventually faded.

But these disappointments were soon eclipsed: that same year, Coleridge made the acquaintance of William Wordsworth, and they embarked on a poetic and philosophical collaboration that would define not only both of their careers but also the artistic legacy of their era.

In the late 1790s the two poets lived near each other in Somerset and would meet to discuss the purpose and potential of poetry. 'Our conversations turned frequently on the two cardinal points of poetry,' Coleridge wrote, 'the power of exciting the sympathy of the reader by a faithful adherence to the truth of nature, and the power of giving the interest of novelty by the modifying colours of imagination.' They determined to publish a joint collection of poems in which Coleridge would focus on 'persons and characters supernatural' while Wordsworth would celebrate 'things of every day'. This project materialised in 1798 as *Lyrical Ballads*, an anthology that included some of the poems for which both men are now best known: Wordsworth's 'Tintern Abbey' and Coleridge's 'The Rime of the Ancient Mariner'.

Lyrical Ballads is credited with bringing Romanticism to Britain. This movement was already flourishing in Germany, and it would ultimately dominate European artistic output until the mid-nineteenth century. Romanticism favoured emotion and imagination over reason and intellect, and tended to celebrate nature, heroism and spiritual experiences. Coleridge, Wordsworth, Southey and Lamb were soon joined by a younger generation of Romantics, including Keats, Byron and Shelley.

An Albatross Around His Neck

'The Rime of the Ancient Mariner', a ballad in seven parts, is Coleridge's longest poem. The mariner of the title detains a man who is on his way to a wedding, and insists on recounting an increasingly terrifying tale of disaster upon the high seas. Gradually the wedding guest is drawn into the frenzied narration of this 'grey-beard loon', for it transpires that thc disaster is entirely self-inflicted. Having been driven south by inclement weather, the mariner's vessel is caught in Antarctic ice. The sudden appearance of an albatross – a symbol of good fortune – helps them escape, but then the mariner does something inexplicably ungrateful: 'With my cross-bow / I shot the Albatross.'

Before long this crime is roundly avenged. The ship finds itself trapped once again, this time on calm, windless waters near the equator, and supplies quite literally dry up: 'Water, water, every where, / Nor any drop to drink.' The sailors rightly blame the mariner for his inauspicious murder of the albatross, and hang the bird about his neck as a sign of his disgrace. The arrival of another ship only compounds the horror, manned as it is by Death and Life-in-Death. They kill the crew but the mariner is forced to spend seven days and nights in a waking, raving nightmare. He eventually understands that it is his eternal curse and punishment to travel from 'land to land' recounting his 'ghastly tale'.

The poem baffled many contemporary readers, and even Wordsworth later wrote that, for all its 'delicate touches of passion' and 'felicity of language', it nevertheless had 'great defects'. For an 1817 reprint, in response to criticism that the poem was hard to follow, Coleridge added dozens of marginal notes explaining the plot: 'The ancient Mariner inhospitably killeth the pious bird of good omen.'

Waking Dreams

Many of Coleridge's poems display a visionary quality that borders on the hallucinogenic, and this is no coincidence. He had since his childhood suffered from health troubles whose symptoms were eased by opium, but by adulthood Coleridge had developed a powerful addiction to the drug that would plague the remainder of his life. He famously composed the vividly exotic 'Kubla Khan' in a fevered state after waking from an opium dream. This poem, like the supernatural 'Christabel', was never completed.

As he fell further into what he called his 'accursed habit' and its attendant depression, Coleridge's life and work suffered considerably. In 1808, he finally separated from his long-suffering wife, leaving her and their three surviving children in the care of Robert Southey. By 1810 Wordsworth had become so frustrated by Coleridge's addiction that the two poets fell out, remaining estranged for over a decade.

Coleridge spent the last eighteen years of his life at the London home of a physician friend, James Gilman, occasionally lecturing on Shakespeare and other poets and repeatedly attempting to give up his opium habit. He died in 1834.

THE RIME OF THE ANCIENT MARINER AND OTHER POEMS

CONTENTS

PART 1:

THE RIME OF THE ANCIENT MARINER, CHRISTABEL AND KUBLA KHAN

THE RIME OF THE ANCIENT MARINER

Part I

An ancient Mariner meeteth three Gallants bidden to a wedding-feast, and detaineth one.

It is an ancient Mariner,
And he stoppeth one of three.
'By thy long grey beard and glittering eye,
Now wherefore stopp'st thou me?

The Bridegroom's doors are opened wide,
And I am next of kin;
The guests are met, the feast is set:
May'st hear the merry din.'

He holds him with his skinny hand,
'There was a ship,' quoth he.
'Hold off! unhand me, grey-beard loon!'
Eftsoons his hand dropt he.

The Wedding-Guest is spell-bound by the eye of the old seafaring man, and constrained to hear his tale.

He holds him with his glittering eye–
The Wedding-Guest stood still,
And listens like a three years' child:
The Mariner hath his will.

The Wedding-Guest sat on a stone:
He cannot choose but hear;
And thus spake on that ancient man,
The bright-eyed Mariner.

'The ship was cheered, the harbour cleared,
Merrily did we drop
Below the kirk, below the hill,
Below the lighthouse top.

The Mariner tells how the ship sailed southward with a good wind and fair weather, till it reached the line.

The Sun came up upon the left,
Out of the sea came he!
And he shone bright, and on the right
Went down into the sea.

Higher and higher every day,
Till over the mast at noon–'
The Wedding-Guest here beat his breast,
For he heard the loud bassoon.

The Wedding-Guest heareth the bridal music; but the Mariner continueth his tale.

The bride hath paced into the hall,
Red as a rose is she;
Nodding their heads before her goes
The merry minstrelsy.

The Wedding-Guest he beat his breast,
Yet he cannot choose but hear;
And thus spake on that ancient man,
The bright-eyed Mariner.

The ship driven by a storm toward the south pole.

'And now the Storm-blast came, and he
Was tyrannous and strong:
He struck with his o'ertaking wings,
And chased us south along.

With sloping masts and dipping prow,
As who pursued with yell and blow
Still treads the shadow of his foe,
And forward bends his head,
The ship drove fast, loud roared the blast,
And southward aye we fled.

And now there came both mist and snow,
And it grew wondrous cold:
And ice, mast-high, came floating by,
As green as emerald.

And through the drifts the snowy clifts
Did send a dismal sheen:
Nor shapes of men nor beasts we ken–
The ice was all between.

The land of ice, and of fearful sounds where no living thing was to be seen.

The ice was here, the ice was there,
The ice was all around:
It cracked and growled, and roared and
howled,
Like noises in a swound!

At length did cross an Albatross,
Thorough the fog it came;
As if it had been a Christian soul,
We hailed it in God's name.

Till a great sea-bird, called the Albatross, came through the snow-fog, and was received with great joy and hospitality.

It ate the food it ne'er had eat,
And round and round it flew.
The ice did split with a thunder-fit;
The helmsman steered us through!

And lo! the Albatross proveth a bird of good omen, and followeth the ship as it returned northward through fog and floating ice.

And a good south wind sprung up behind;
The Albatross did follow,
And every day, for food or play,
Came to the mariner's hollo!

In mist or cloud, on mast or shroud,
It perched for vespers nine;
Whiles all the night, through fog-smoke white,
Glimmered the white Moon-shine.'

The ancient Mariner inhospitably killeth the pious bird of good omen.

'God save thee, ancient Mariner!
From the fiends, that plague thee thus!–
Why look'st thou so?'– With my cross-bow
I shot the Albatross.

Part II

'The Sun now rose upon the right:
Out of the sea came he,
Still hid in mist, and on the left
Went down into the sea.

And the good south wind still blew behind,
But no sweet bird did follow,
Nor any day for food or play
Came to the mariners' hollo!

His shipmates cry out against the ancient Mariner, for killing the bird of good luck.

And I had done a hellish thing,
And it would work 'em woe:
For all averred, I had killed the bird
That made the breeze to blow.
Ah wretch! said they, the bird to slay,
That made the breeze to blow!

Nor dim nor red, like God's own head,
The glorious Sun uprist:
Then all averred, I had killed the bird
That brought the fog and mist.
'Twas right, said they, such birds to slay,
That bring the fog and mist.

But when the fog cleared off, they justify the same, and thus make themselves accomplices in the crime.

The fair breeze blew, the white foam flew,
The furrow followed free;
We were the first that ever burst
Into that silent sea.

The fair breeze continues; the ship enters the Pacific Ocean, and sails northward, even till it reaches the Line. The ship hath been suddenly becalmed.

Down dropt the breeze, the sails dropt
  down,
'Twas sad as sad could be;
And we did speak only to break
The silence of the sea!

All in a hot and copper sky,
The bloody Sun at noon,
Right up above the mast did stand,
No bigger than the Moon.

Day after day, day after day,
We stuck, nor breath nor motion;
As idle as a painted ship
Upon a painted ocean.

Water, water, every where,
And all the boards did shrink;
Water, water, every where,
Nor any drop to drink.

And the Albatross begins to be avenged.

The very deep did rot: O Christ!
That ever this should be!
Yea, slimy things did crawl with legs
Upon the slimy sea.

About, about, in reel and rout
The death-fires danced at night;
The water, like a witch's oils,
Burnt green, and blue and white.

A Spirit had followed them; one of the invisible inhabitants of this planet, neither departed souls nor angels; concerning whom the learned Jew, Josephus, and the Platonic Constantinopolitan, Michael Psellus, may be consulted. They are very numerous, and there is no climate or element without one or more.

And some in dreams assuréd were
Of the Spirit that plagued us so;
Nine fathom deep he had followed us
From the land of mist and snow.

And every tongue, through utter drought,
Was withered at the root;
We could not speak, no more than if
We had been choked with soot.

The shipmates, in their sore distress, would fain throw the whole guilt on the ancient Mariner: in sign whereof they hang the dead sea-bird round his neck.

Ah! well a-day! what evil looks
Had I from old and young!
Instead of the cross, the Albatross
About my neck was hung.

PART III

'There passed a weary time. Each throat
Was parched, and glazed each eye.
A weary time! a weary time!
How glazed each weary eye,
When looking westward, I beheld
A something in the sky.

The ancient Mariner beholdeth a sign in the element afar off.

At first it seemed a little speck,
And then it seemed a mist;
It moved and moved, and took at last
A certain shape, I wist.

A speck, a mist, a shape, I wist!
And still it neared and neared:
As if it dodged a water-sprite,
It plunged and tacked and veered.

At its nearer approach, it seemeth him to be a ship; and at a dear ransom he freeth his speech from the bonds of thirst.

With throats unslaked, with black lips
  baked,
We could nor laugh nor wail;
Through utter drought all dumb we stood!
I bit my arm, I sucked the blood,
And cried, A sail! a sail!

With throats unslaked, with black lips
  baked,
Agape they heard me call:
Gramercy! they for joy did grin,
And all at once their breath drew in,
As they were drinking all.

A flash of joy;

And horror follows. For can it be a ship that comes onward without wind or tide?

See! see! (I cried) she tacks no more!
Hither to work us weal;
Without a breeze, without a tide,
She steadies with upright keel!

The western wave was all a-flame.
The day was well nigh done!
Almost upon the western wave
Bested the broad bright Sun;
When that strange shape drove suddenly
Betwixt us and the Sun.

It seemeth him but the skeleton of a ship.

And straight the Sun was flecked with bars,
(Heaven's Mother send us grace!)
As if through a dungeon-grate he peered
With broad and burning face.

Alas! (thought I, and my heart beat loud)
How fast she nears and nears!
Are those *her* sails that glance in the Sun,
Like restless gossameres?

And its ribs are seen as bars on the face of the setting Sun. The Spectre-Woman and her Death-mate, and no other on board the skeleton ship. Like vessel, like crew!

Are those *her* ribs through which the Sun
Did peer, as through a grate?
And is that Woman all her crew?
Is that a Death? and are there two?
Is Death that woman's mate?

Her lips were red, *her* looks were free,
Her locks were yellow as gold:
Her skin was as white as leprosy,
The Night-mare Life-in-Death was she,
Who thicks man's blood with cold.

The naked hulk alongside came,
And the twain were casting dice;
'The game is done! I've won! I've won!'
Quoth she, and whistles thrice.

Death and Life-in-Death have diced for the ship's crew, and she (the latter) winneth the ancient Mariner.

The Sun's rim dips: the stars rush out:
At one stride comes the dark;
With far-heard whisper, o'er the sea,
Off shot the spectre-bark.

No twilight within the courts of the Sun.

We listened and looked sideways up!
Fear at my heart, as at a cup,
My life-blood seemed to sip!
The stars were dim, and thick the night,
The steersman's face by his lamp
  gleamed white;
From the sails the dew did drip–
Till clomb above the eastern bar
The hornéd Moon, with one bright star
Within the nether tip.

At the rising of the Moon.

One after one, by the star-dogged Moon,
Too quick for groan or sigh,
Each turned his face with a ghastly pang,
And cursed me with his eye.

One after another,

Four times fifty living men,
(And I heard nor sigh nor groan)
With heavy thump, a lifeless lump,
They dropped down one by one.

His shipmates drop down dead.

The souls did from their bodies fly,–
They fled to bliss or woe!
And every soul, it passed me by,
Like the whizz of my cross-bow!

But Life-in-Death begins her work on the ancient Mariner.

Part IV

The Wedding-Guest feareth that a Spirit is talking to him;

'I fear thee, ancient Mariner!
I fear thy skinny hand!
And thou art long, and lank, and brown,
As is the ribbed sea-sand.

I fear thee and thy glittering eye,
And thy skinny hand, so brown.'—

But the ancient Mariner assureth him of his bodily life, and proceedeth to relate his horrible penance.

'Fear not, fear not, thou Wedding-Guest!
This body dropt not down.

Alone, alone, all, all alone,
Alone on a wide wide sea!
And never a saint took pity on
My soul in agony.

He despiseth the creatures of the calm,

The many men, so beautiful!
And they all dead did lie:
And a thousand thousand slimy things
Lived on; and so did I.

And envieth that they should live, and so many lie dead.

I looked upon the rotting sea,
And drew my eyes away;
I looked upon the rotting deck,
And there the dead men lay.

I looked to heaven, and tried to pray;
But or ever a prayer had gusht,
A wicked whisper came, and made
My heart as dry as dust.

I closed my lids, and kept them close,
And the balls like pulses beat;
For the sky and the sea, and the sea and the sky
Lay like a load on my weary eye,
And the dead were at my feet.

The cold sweat melted from their limbs,
Nor rot nor reek did they:
The look with which they looked on me
Had never passed away.

But the curse liveth for him in the eye of the dead men.

An orphan's curse would drag to hell
A spirit from on high;
But oh! more horrible than that
Is the curse in a dead man's eye!
Seven days, seven nights, I saw that curse,
And yet I could not die.

The moving Moon went up the sky,
And no where did abide:
Softly she was going up,
And a star or two beside–

In his loneliness and fixedness he yearneth towards the journeying Moon, and the stars that still sojourn, yet still move onward; and every where the blue sky belongs to them, and is their appointed rest, and their native country and their own natural homes, which they enter unannounced, as lords that are certainly expected and yet there is a silent joy at their arrival.

Her beams bemocked the sultry main,
Like April hoar-frost spread;
But where the ship's huge shadow lay,
The charméd water burnt alway
A still and awful red.

By the light of the Moon he beholdeth God's creatures of the great calm.

Beyond the shadow of the ship,
I watched the water-snakes:
They moved in tracks of shining white,
And when they reared, the elfish light
Fell off in hoary flakes.

Within the shadow of the ship
I watched their rich attire:
Blue, glossy green, and velvet black,
They coiled and swam; and every track
Was a flash of golden fire.

Their beauty and their happiness.

He blesseth them in his heart.

O happy living things! no tongue
Their beauty might declare:
A spring of love gushed from my heart,
And I blessed them unaware:
Sure my kind saint took pity on me,
And I blessed them unaware.

The spell begins to break.

The self-same moment I could pray;
And from my neck so free
The Albatross fell off, and sank
Like lead into the sea.

PART V

'Oh sleep! it is a gentle thing,
Beloved from pole to pole!
To Mary Queen the praise be given!
She sent the gentle sleep from Heaven,
That slid into my soul.

The silly buckets on the deck,
That had so long remained,
I dreamt that they were filled with dew;
And when I awoke, it rained.

By grace of the holy Mother, the ancient Mariner is refreshed with rain.

My lips were wet, my throat was cold,
My garments all were dank;
Sure I had drunken in my dreams,
And still my body drank.

I moved, and could not feel my limbs:
I was so light–almost
I thought that I had died in sleep,
And was a blessèd ghost.

And soon I heard a roaring wind:
It did not come anear;
But with its sound it shook the sails,
That were so thin and sere.

He heareth sounds and seeth strange sights and commotions in the sky and the element.

The upper air burst into life!
And a hundred fire-flags sheen,
To and fro they were hurried about!
And to and fro, and in and out,
The wan stars danced between.

And the coming wind did roar more loud,
And the sails did sigh like sedge;
And the rain poured down from one black
  cloud;
The Moon was at its edge.

The thick black cloud was cleft, and still
The Moon was at its side:
Like waters shot from some high crag,

The lightning fell with never a jag,
A river steep and wide.

The bodies of the ship's crew are inspired and the ship moves on;

The loud wind never reached the ship,
Yet now the ship moved on!
Beneath the lightning and the Moon
The dead men gave a groan.

They groaned, they stirred, they all uprose,
Nor spake, nor moved their eyes;
It had been strange, even in a dream,
To have seen those dead men rise.

The helmsman steered, the ship moved on;
Yet never a breeze up-blew;
The mariners all 'gan work the ropes,
Where they were wont to do;
They raised their limbs like lifeless tools—
We were a ghastly crew.

The body of my brother's son
Stood by me, knee to knee:
The body and I pulled at one rope,
But he said nought to me.

But not by the souls of the men, nor by dæmons of earth or middle air, but by a blessed troop of angelic spirits, sent down by the invocation of the guardian saint.

'I fear thee, ancient Mariner!'
Be calm, thou Wedding-Guest!
'Twas not those souls that fled in pain,
Which to their corses came again,
But a troop of spirits blest:

For when it dawned—they dropped their arms,
And clustered round the mast;
Sweet sounds rose slowly through their mouths,
And from their bodies passed.

Around, around, flew each sweet sound,
Then darted to the Sun;
Slowly the sounds came back again,
Now mixed, now one by one.

Sometimes a-dropping from the sky
I heard the sky-lark sing;
Sometimes all little birds that are,
How they seemed to fill the sea and air
With their sweet jargoning!

And now 'twas like all instruments,
Now like a lonely flute;
And now it is an angel's song,
That makes the heavens be mute.

It ceased; yet still the sails made on
A pleasant noise till noon,
A noise like of a hidden brook
In the leafy month of June,
That to the sleeping woods all night
Singeth a quiet tune.

Till noon we quietly sailed on,
Yet never a breeze did breathe:
Slowly and smoothly went the ship,
Moved onward from beneath.

Under the keel nine fathom deep,
From the land of mist and snow,
The spirit slid: and it was he
That made the ship to go.
The sails at noon left off their tune,
And the ship stood still also.

The lonesome Spirit from the south-pole carries on the ship as far as the Line, in obedience to the angelic troop, but still requireth vengeance.

The Sun, right up above the mast,
Had fixed her to the ocean:
But in a minute she 'gan stir,
With a short uneasy motion–
Backwards and forwards half her length
With a short uneasy motion.

Then like a pawing horse let go,
She made a sudden bound:
It flung the blood into my head,
And I fell down in a swound.

The Polar Spirit's fellow-dæmons, the invisible inhabitants of the element, take part in his wrong; and two of them relate, one to the other, that penance long and heavy for the ancient Mariner hath been accorded to the Polar Spirit, who returneth southward.

How long in that same fit I lay,
I have not to declare;
But ere my living life returned,
I heard and in my soul discerned
Two voices in the air.

'Is it he?' quoth one, 'Is this the man?
By him who died on cross,
With his cruel bow he laid full low
The harmless Albatross.

The spirit who bideth by himself
In the land of mist and snow,
He loved the bird that loved the man
Who shot him with his bow.'

The other was a softer voice,
As soft as honey-dew:
Quoth he, 'The man hath penance done,
And penance more will do.'

Part VI

FIRST VOICE

'But tell me, tell me! speak again,
Thy soft response renewing–
What makes that ship drive on so fast?
What is the ocean doing?'

SECOND VOICE

'Still as a slave before his lord,
The ocean hath no blast;
His great bright eye most silently
Up to the Moon is cast–

If he may know which way to go;
For she guides him smooth or grim.
See, brother, see! how graciously
She looketh down on him.'

FIRST VOICE

'But why drives on that ship so fast,
Without or wave or wind?'

The Mariner hath been cast into a trance; for the angelic power causeth the vessel to drive northward faster than human life could endure.

SECOND VOICE

'The air is cut away before,
And closes from behind.
Fly, brother, fly! more high, more high!
Or we shall be belated:
For slow and slow that ship will go,
When the Mariner's trance is abated.'

The supernatural motion is retarded; the Mariner awakes, and his penance begins anew.

I woke, and we were sailing on
As in a gentle weather:
'Twas night, calm night, the moon was high;
The dead men stood together.

All stood together on the deck,
For a charnel-dungeon fitter:
All fixed on me their stony eyes,
That in the Moon did glitter.

The pang, the curse, with which they died,
Had never passed away:
I could not draw my eyes from theirs,
Nor turn them up to pray.

The curse is finally expiated.

And now this spell was snapt: once more
I viewed the ocean green,
And looked far forth, yet little saw
Of what had else been seen–

Like one, that on a lonesome road
Doth walk in fear and dread,
And having once turned round walks on,
And turns no more his head;
Because he knows, a frightful fiend
Doth close behind him tread.

But soon there breathed a wind on me,
Nor sound nor motion made:
Its path was not upon the sea,
In ripple or in shade.

It raised my hair, it fanned my cheek
Like a meadow-gale of spring–

It mingled strangely with my fears,
Yet it felt like a welcoming.

Swiftly, swiftly flew the ship,
Yet she sailed softly too:
Sweetly, sweetly blew the breeze—
On me alone it blew.

Oh! dream of joy! is this indeed
The light-house top I see?
Is this the hill? is this the kirk?
Is this mine own countree?

And the ancient Mariner beholdeth his native country.

We drifted o'er the harbour-bar,
And I with sobs did pray—
O let me be awake, my God!
Or let me sleep alway.

The harbour-bay was clear as glass,
So smoothly it was strewn!
And on the bay the moonlight lay,
And the shadow of the Moon.

The rock shone bright, the kirk no less,
That stands above the rock:
The moonlight steeped in silentness
The steady weathercock.

And the bay was white with silent light,
Till rising from the same,
Full many shapes, that shadows were,
In crimson colours came.

The angelic spirits leave the dead bodies,

A little distance from the prow
Those crimson shadows were:

And appear in their own forms of light.

I turned my eyes upon the deck–
Oh, Christ! what saw I there!

Each corse lay flat, lifeless and flat,
And, by the holy rood!
A man all light, a seraph-man,
On every corse there stood.

This seraph-band, each waved his hand:
It was a heavenly sight!
They stood as signals to the land,
Each one a lovely light;

This seraph-band, each waved his hand,
No voice did they impart–
No voice; but oh! the silence sank
Like music on my heart.

But soon I heard the dash of oars,
I heard the Pilot's cheer;
My head was turned perforce away,
And I saw a boat appear.

The Pilot and the Pilot's boy,
I heard them coming fast:
Dear Lord in Heaven! it was a joy
The dead men could not blast.

I saw a third–I heard his voice:
It is the Hermit good!
He singeth loud his godly hymns
That he makes in the wood.
He'll shrieve my soul, he'll wash away
The Albatross's blood.

Part VII

The Hermit of the Wood,

'This Hermit good lives in that wood
Which slopes down to the sea.
How loudly his sweet voice he rears!
He loves to talk with marineres
That come from a far countree.

He kneels at morn, and noon, and eve–
He hath a cushion plump:
It is the moss that wholly hides
The rotted old oak-stump.

The skiff-boat neared: I heard them talk,
'Why, this is strange, I trow!
Where are those lights so many and fair,
That signal made but now?'

Approacheth the ship with wonder.

'Strange, by my faith!' the Hermit said–
'And they answered not our cheer!
The planks looked warped! and see those sails,
How thin they are and sere!
I never saw aught like to them,
Unless perchance it were

Brown skeletons of leaves that lag
My forest-brook along;
When the ivy-tod is heavy with snow,
And the owlet whoops to the wolf below,
That eats the she-wolf's young.'

'Dear Lord! it hath a fiendish look–
(The Pilot made reply)
I am a-feared'–'Push on, push on!'
Said the Hermit cheerily.

The boat came closer to the ship,
But I nor spake nor stirred;
The boat came close beneath the ship,
And straight a sound was heard.

The ship suddenly sinketh.

Under the water it rumbled on,
Still louder and more dread:
It reached the ship, it split the bay;
The ship went down like lead.

The ancient Mariner is saved in the Pilot's boat.

Stunned by that loud and dreadful sound,
Which sky and ocean smote,
Like one that hath been seven days
  drowned
My body lay afloat;
But swift as dreams, myself I found
Within the Pilot's boat.

Upon the whirl, where sank the ship,
The boat spun round and round;
And all was still, save that the hill
Was telling of the sound.

I moved my lips–the Pilot shrieked
And fell down in a fit;
The holy Hermit raised his eyes,
And prayed where he did sit.

I took the oars: the Pilot's boy,
Who now doth crazy go,
Laughed loud and long, and all the while
His eyes went to and fro.
'Ha! ha!' quoth he, 'full plain I see.
The Devil knows how to row.'

And now, all in my own countree,
I stood on the firm land!
The Hermit stepped forth from the boat,
And scarcely he could stand.

'O shrieve me, shrieve me, holy man!'
The Hermit crossed his brow.
'Say quick,' quoth he, 'I bid thee say–
What manner of man art thou?'

The ancient Mariner earnestly entreateth the Hermit to shrieve him; and the penance of life falls on him.

Forthwith this frame of mine was wrenched
With a woful agony,
Which forced me to begin my tale;
And then it left me free.

Since then, at an uncertain hour,
That agony returns:
And till my ghastly tale is told,
This heart within me burns.

And ever and anon throughout his future life an agony constraineth him to travel from land to land;

I pass, like night, from land to land;
I have strange power of speech;
That moment that his face I see,
I know the man that must hear me:
To him my tale I teach.

What loud uproar bursts from that door!
The wedding-guests are there:
But in the garden-bower the bride
And bride-maids singing are:
And hark the little vesper bell,
Which biddeth me to prayer!

O Wedding-Guest! this soul hath been
Alone on a wide wide sea:

So lonely 'twas, that God himself
Scarce seemèd there to be.

O sweeter than the marriage-feast,
'Tis sweeter far to me,
To walk together to the kirk
With a goodly company!–

To walk together to the kirk,
And all together pray,
While each to his great Father bends,
Old men, and babes, and loving friends
And youths and maidens gay!

And to teach, by his own example, love and reverence to all things that God made and loveth.

Farewell, farewell! but this I tell
To thee, thou Wedding-Guest!
He prayeth well, who loveth well
Both man and bird and beast.

He prayeth best, who loveth best
All things both great and small;
For the dear God who loveth us,
He made and loveth all.

The Mariner, whose eye is bright,
Whose beard with age is hoar,
Is gone: and now the Wedding-Guest
Turned from the bridegroom's door.

He went like one that hath been stunned,
And is of sense forlorn:
A sadder and a wiser man,
He rose the morrow morn.

1797–1798.

CHRISTABEL

Part I

'Tis the middle of night by the castle clock,
And the owls have awakened the crowing cock;
Tu–whit!–Tu–whoo!
And hark, again! the crowing cock,
How drowsily it crew.

Sir Leoline, the Baron rich,
Hath a toothless mastiff bitch;
From her kennel beneath the rock
She maketh answer to the clock,
Four for the quarters, and twelve for the hour;
Ever and aye, by shine and shower,
Sixteen short howls, not over loud;
Some say, she sees my lady's shroud.

Is the night chilly and dark?
The night is chilly, but not dark.
The thin gray cloud is spread on high,
It covers but not hides the sky.
The moon is behind, and at the full;

And yet she looks both small and dull.
The night is chill, the cloud is gray:
'Tis a month before the month of May,
And the Spring comes slowly up this way.

The lovely lady, Christabel,
Whom her father loves so well,
What makes her in the wood so late,
A furlong from the castle gate?
She had dreams all yesternight
Of her own betrothéd knight;
And she in the midnight wood will pray
For the weal of her lover that's far away.

She stole along, she nothing spoke,
The sighs she heaved were soft and low,
And naught was green upon the oak
But moss and rarest misletoe:
She kneels beneath the huge oak tree,
And in silence prayeth she.

The lady sprang up suddenly,
The lovely lady, Christabel!
It moaned as near, as near can be,
But what it is she cannot tell.–
On the other side it seems to be,
Of the huge, broad-breasted, old oak tree.

The night is chill; the forest bare;
Is it the wind that moaneth bleak?
There is not wind enough in the air
To move away the ringlet curl
From the lovely lady's cheek–

There is not wind enough to twirl
The one red leaf, the last of its clan,
That dances as often as dance it can,
Hanging so light, and hanging so high,
On the topmost twig that looks up at the sky.

Hush, beating heart of Christabel!
Jesu, Maria, shield her well!
She folded her arms beneath her cloak,
And stole to the other side of the oak.
    What sees she there?

There she sees a damsel bright,
Drest in a silken robe of white,
That shadowy in the moonlight shone:
The neck that made that white robe wan,
Her stately neck, and arms were bare;
Her blue-veined feet unsandal'd were,
And wildly glittered here and there
The gems entangled in her hair.
I guess, 'twas frightful there to see
A lady so richly clad as she–
Beautiful exceedingly!

Mary mother, save me now!
(Said Christabel,) And who art thou?

The lady strange made answer meet,
And her voice was faint and sweet:–
Have pity on my sore distress,
I scarce can speak for weariness:
Stretch forth thy hand, and have no fear!
Said Christabel, How camest thou here?
And the lady, whose voice was faint and sweet,
Did thus pursue her answer meet:–

My sire is of a noble line,
And my name is Geraldine:
Five warriors seized me yestermorn,
Me, even me, a maid forlorn:
They choked my cries with force and fright,
And tied me on a palfrey white.
The palfrey was as fleet as wind,
And they rode furiously behind.
They spurred amain, their steeds were white:
And once we crossed the shade of night.
As sure as Heaven shall rescue me,
I have no thought what men they be;
Nor do I know how long it is
(For I have lain entranced I wis)
Since one, the tallest of the five,
Took me from the palfrey's back,
A weary woman, scarce alive.
Some muttered words his comrades spoke:
Ha placed me underneath this oak;
He swore they would return with haste;
Whither they went I cannot tell–
I thought I heard, some minutes past,
Sounds as of a castle bell.
Stretch forth thy hand (thus ended she),
And help a wretched maid to flee.

Then Christabel stretched forth her hand,
And comforted fair Geraldine:
O well, bright dame! may you command
The service of Sir Leoline;
And gladly our stout chivalry
Will he send forth and friends withal
To guide and guard you safe and free
Home to your noble father's hall.

She rose: and forth with steps they passed
That strove to be, and were not, fast.
Her gracious stars the lady blest,
And thus spake on sweet Christabel:
All our household are at rest,
The hall as silent as the cell;
Sir Leoline is weak in health,
And may not well awakened be,
But we will move as if in stealth,
And I beseech your courtesy,
This night, to share your couch with me.

They crossed the moat, and Christabel
Took the key that fitted well;
A little door she opened straight,
All in the middle of the gate;
The gate that was ironed within and without,
Where an army in battle array had marched out.
The lady sank, belike through pain,
And Christabel with might and main
Lifted her up, a weary weight,
Over the threshold of the gate:
Then the lady rose again,
And moved, as she were not in pain.

So free from danger, free from fear,
They crossed the court: right glad they were.
And Christabel devoutly cried
To the lady by her side,
'Praise we the Virgin all divine
Who hath rescued thee from thy distress!'
'Alas, alas!' said Geraldine,
'I cannot speak for weariness.'
So free from danger, free from fear,
They crossed the court: right glad they were.

Outside her kennel, the mastiff old
Lay fast asleep, in moonshine cold.
The mastiff old did not awake,
Yet she an angry moan did make!
And what can ail the mastiff bitch?
Never till now she uttered yell
Beneath the eye of Christabel.
Perhaps it is the owlet's scritch:
For what can ail the mastiff bitch?

They passed the hall, that echoes still,
Pass as lightly as you will!
The brands were flat, the brands were dying,
Amid their own white ashes lying;
But when the lady passed, there came
A tongue of light, a fit of flame;
And Christabel saw the lady's eye,
And nothing else saw she thereby,
Save the boss of the shield of Sir Leoline tall,
Which hung in a murky old niche in the wall.
O softly tread, said Christabel,
My father seldom sleepeth well.

Sweet Christabel her feet doth bare,
And jealous of the listening air
They steal their way from stair to stair,
Now in glimmer, and now in gloom,
And now they pass the Baron's room,
As still as death, with stifled breath!
And now have reached her chamber door;
And now doth Geraldine press down
The rushes of the chamber floor.

The moon shines dim in the open air,
And not a moonbeam enters here.

But they without its light can see
The chamber carved so curiously,
Carved with figures strange and sweet,
All made out of the carver's brain,
For a lady's chamber meet:
The lamp with twofold silver chain
Is fastened to an angel's feet.
The silver lamp burns dead and dim;
But Christabel the lamp will trim.
She trimmed the lamp, and made it bright,
And left it swinging to and fro,
While Geraldine, in wretched plight,
Sank down upon the floor below.

'O weary lady, Geraldine,
I pray you, drink this cordial wine!
It is a wine of virtuous powers;
My mother made it of wild flowers.'

'And will your mother pity me,
Who am a maiden most forlorn?'
Christabel answered—'Woe is me!
She died the hour that I was born.
I have heard the grey-haired friar tell
How on her death-bed she did say,
That she should hear the castle-bell
Strike twelve upon my wedding-day.
O mother dear! that thou wert here!'
'I would,' said Geraldine, 'she were!'

But soon with altered voice, said she—
'Off, wandering mother! Peak and pine!
I have power to bid thee flee.'
Alas! what ails poor Geraldine?
Why stares she with unsettled eye?

Can she the bodiless dead espy?
And why with hollow voice cries she,
'Off, woman, off! this hour is mine–
Though thou her guardian spirit be,
Off, woman, off! 'tis given to me.'

Then Christabel knelt by the lady's side,
And raised to heaven her eyes so blue–
'Alas!' said she, 'this ghastly ride–
Dear lady! it hath wildered you!'
The lady wiped her moist cold brow,
And faintly said, ''tis over now!'

Again the wild-flower wine she drank:
Her fair large eyes 'gan glitter bright,
And from the floor whereon she sank,
The lofty lady stood upright:
She was most beautiful to see,
Like a lady of a far countrèe.

And thus the lofty lady spake–
'All they who live in the upper sky,
Do love you, holy Christabel!
And you love them, and for their sake
And for the good which me befel,
Even I in my degree will try,
Fair maiden, to requite you well.
But now unrobe yourself; for I
Must pray, ere yet in bed I lie.'

Quoth Christabel, 'So let it be!'
And as the lady bade, did she.
Her gentle limbs did she undress,
And lay down in her loveliness.

But through her brain of weal and woe
So many thoughts moved to and fro,
That vain it were her lids to close;
So half-way from the bed she rose,
And on her elbow did recline
To look at the lady Geraldine.

Beneath the lamp the lady bowed,
And slowly rolled her eyes around;
Then drawing in her breath aloud,
Like one that shuddered, she unbound
The cincture from beneath her breast:
Her silken robe, and inner vest,
Dropt to her feet, and full in view,
Behold! her bosom and half her side–
A sight to dream of, not to tell!
O shield her! shield sweet Christabel!

Yet Geraldine nor speaks nor stirs;
Ah! what a stricken look was hers!
Deep from within she seems half-way
To lift some weight with sick assay,
And eyes the maid and seeks delay;
Then suddenly, as one defied,
Collects herself in scorn and pride,
And lay down by the Maiden's side!–
And in her arms the maid she took,
Ah wel-a-day!
And with low voice and doleful look
These words did say:
'In the touch of this bosom there worketh a spell,
Which is lord of thy utterance, Christabel!
Thou knowest to-night, and wilt know to-morrow,
This mark of my shame, this seal of my sorrow;
But vainly thou warrest,

For this is alone in
Thy power to declare,
That in the dim forest
Thou heard'st a low moaning,
And found'st a bright lady, surpassingly fair;
And didst bring her home with thee in love and in charity,
To shield her and shelter her from the damp air.'

The Conclusion to Part I

It was a lovely sight to see
The lady Christabel, when she
Was praying at the old oak tree.
Amid the jaggéd shadows
Of mossy leafless boughs,
Kneeling in the moonlight,
To make her gentle vows;
Her slender palms together prest,
Heaving sometimes on her breast;
Her face resigned to bliss or bale–
Her face, oh call it fair not pale,
And both blue eyes more bright than clear,
Each about to have a tear.

With open eyes (ah woe is me!)
Asleep, and dreaming fearfully,
Fearfully dreaming, yet, I wis,
Dreaming that alone, which is–
O sorrow and shame! Can this be she,
The lady, who knelt at the old oak tree?
And lo! the worker of these harms,
That holds the maiden in her arms,
Seems to slumber still and mild,
As a mother with her child.

A star hath set, a star hath risen,
O Geraldine! since arms of thine
Have been the lovely lady's prison.
O Geraldine! one hour was thine–
Thou'st had thy will! By tairn and rill,
The night-birds all that hour were still.
But now they are jubilant anew,
From cliff and tower, tu–whoo! tu–whoo!
Tu–whoo! tu–whoo! from wood and fell!

And see! the lady Christabel
Gathers herself from out her trance;
Her limbs relax, her countenance
Grows sad and soft; the smooth thin lids
Close o'er her eyes; and tears she sheds–
Large tears that leave the lashes bright!
And oft the while she seems to smile
As infants at a sudden light!
Yea, she doth smile, and she doth weep,
Like a youthful hermitess,
Beauteous in a wilderness,
Who, praying always, prays in sleep.
And, if she move unquietly,
Perchance, 'tis but the blood so free
Comes back and tingles in her feet.
No doubt, she hath a vision sweet.
What if her guardian spirit 'twere,
What if she knew her mother near?
But this she knows, in joys and woes,
That saints will aid if men will call:
For the blue sky bends over all!

1797.

Part II

'Each matin bell, the Baron saith,
Knells us back to a world of death.'
These words Sir Leoline first said,
When he rose and found his lady dead:
These words Sir Leoline will say
Many a morn to his dying day!

And hence the custom and law began
That still at dawn the sacristan,
Who duly pulls the heavy bell,
Five and forty beads must tell
Between each stroke–a warning knell,
Which not a soul can choose but hear
From Bratha Head to Wyndermere.

Saith Bracy the bard, 'So let it knell!
And let the drowsy sacristan
Still count as slowly as he can!
There is no lack of such, I ween,
As well fill up the space between.
In Langdale Pike and Witch's Lair,
And Dungeon-ghyll so foully rent,
With ropes of rock and bells of air
Three sinful sextons' ghosts are pent,
Who all give back, one after t'other,
The death-note to their living brother;
And oft too, by the knell offended,
Just as their one! two! three! is ended,
The devil mocks the doleful tale
With a merry peal from Borodale.'

The air is still! through mist and cloud
That merry peal comes ringing loud;

And Geraldine shakes off her dread,
And rises lightly from the bed;
Puts on her silken vestments white,
And tricks her hair in lovely plight,
And nothing doubting of her spell
Awakens the lady Christabel.
'Sleep you, sweet lady Christabel?
I trust that you have rested well.'

And Christabel awoke and spied
The same who lay down by her side–
O rather say, the same whom she
Raised up beneath the old oak tree!
Nay, fairer yet! and yet more fair!
For she belike hath drunken deep
Of all the blessedness of sleep!
And while she spake, her looks, her air
Such gentle thankfulness declare,
That (so it seemed) her girded vests
Grew tight beneath her heaving breasts.
'Sure I have sinn'd!' said Christabel,
'Now heaven be praised if all be well!'
And in low faltering tones, yet sweet,
Did she the lofty lady greet
With such perplexity of mind
As dreams too lively leave behind.

So quickly she rose, and quickly arrayed
Her maiden limbs, and having prayed
That He, who on the cross did groan,
Might wash away her sins unknown,
She forthwith led fair Geraldine
To meet her sire, Sir Leoline.

The lovely maid and the lady tall
Are pacing both into the hall,
And pacing on through page and groom,
Enter the Baron's presence-room.

The Baron rose, and while he prest
His gentle daughter to his breast,
With cheerful wonder in his eyes
The lady Geraldine espies,
And gave such welcome to the same,
As might beseem so bright a dame!

But when he heard the lady's tale,
And when she told her father's name,
Why waxed Sir Leoline so pale,
Murmuring o'er the name again,
Lord Roland de Vaux of Tryermaine?
Alas! they had been friends in youth;
But whispering tongues can poison truth;
And constancy lives in realms above;
And life is thorny; and youth is vain;
And to be wroth with one we love
Doth work like madness in the brain.
And thus it chanced, as I divine,
With Roland and Sir Leoline.
Each spake words of high disdain
And insult to his heart's best brother:
They parted–ne'er to meet again!
But never either found another
To free the hollow heart from paining–
They stood aloof, the scars remaining,
Like cliffs which had been rent asunder;
A dreary sea now flows between;–
But neither heat, nor frost, nor thunder,

Shall wholly do away, I ween,
The marks of that which once hath been.

Sir Leoline, a moment's space,
Stood gazing on the damsel's face:
And the youthful Lord of Tryermaine
Came back upon his heart again.

O then the Baron forgot his age,
His noble heart swelled high with rage;
He swore by the wounds in Jesu's side
He would proclaim it far and wide,
With trump and solemn heraldry,
That they, who thus had wronged the dame,
Were base as spotted infamy!
'And if they dare deny the same,
My herald shall appoint a week,
And let the recreant traitors seek
My tourney court–that there and then
I may dislodge their reptile souls
From the bodies and forms of men!'
He spake: his eye in lightning rolls!
For the lady was ruthlessly seized; and he kenned
In the beautiful lady the child of his friend!

And now the tears were on his face,
And fondly in his arms he took
Fair Geraldine, who met the embrace,
Prolonging it with joyous look.
Which when she viewed, a vision fell
Upon the soul of Christabel,
The vision of fear, the touch and pain!
She shrunk and shuddered, and saw again–

(Ah, woe is me! Was it for thee,
Thou gentle maid! such sights to see?)
Again she saw that bosom old,
Again she felt that bosom cold,
And drew in her breath with a hissing sound:
Whereat the Knight turned wildly round,
And nothing saw, but his own sweet maid
With eyes upraised, as one that prayed.

The touch, the sight, had passed away,
And in its stead that vision blest,
Which comforted her after-rest
While in the lady's arms she lay,
Had put a rapture in her breast,
And on her lips and o'er her eyes
Spread smiles like light!
With new surprise,
'What ails then my belovéd child?'
The Baron said–His daughter mild
Made answer, 'All will yet be well!'
I ween, she had no power to tell
Aught else: so mighty was the spell.

Yet he, who saw this Geraldine,
Had deemed her sure a thing divine:
Such sorrow with such grace she blended,
As if she feared she had offended
Sweet Christabel, that gentle maid!
And with such lowly tones she prayed
She might be sent without delay
Home to her father's mansion.
'Nay!
Nay, by my soul!' said Leoline.

'Ho! Bracy the bard, the charge be thine!
Go thou, with music sweet and loud,
And take two steeds with trappings proud,
And take the youth whom thou lov'st best
To bear thy harp, and learn thy song,
And clothe you both in solemn vest,
And over the mountains haste along,
Lest wandering folk, that are abroad,
Detain you on the valley road.
And when he has crossed the Irthing flood,
My merry bard! he hastes, he hastes
Up Knorren Moor, through Halegarth Wood,
And reaches soon that castle good
Which stands and threatens Scotland's wastes.

'Bard Bracy! bard Bracy! your horses are fleet,
Ye must ride up the hall, your music so sweet,
More loud than your horses' echoing feet!
And loud and loud to Lord Roland call,
Thy daughter is safe in Langdale hall!
Thy beautiful daughter is safe and free–
Sir Leoline greets thee thus through me!
He bids thee come without delay
With all thy numerous array
And take thy lovely daughter home:
And he will meet thee on the way
With all his numerous array
White with their panting palfreys' foam:
And, by mine honour! I will say,
That I repent me of the day
When I spake words of fierce disdain
To Roland de Vaux of Tryermaine!–
–For since that evil hour hath flown,

Many a summer's sun hath shone;
Yet ne'er found I a friend again
Like Roland de Vaux of Tryermaine.'

The lady fell, and clasped his knees,
Her face upraised, her eyes o'erflowing;
And Bracy replied, with faltering voice,
His gracious hail on all bestowing!–
'Thy words, thou sire of Christabel,
Are sweeter than my harp can tell;
Yet might I gain a boon of thee,
This day my journey should not be,
So strange a dream hath come to me,
That I had vowed with music loud
To clear yon wood from thing unblest,
Warned by a vision in my rest!
For in my sleep I saw that dove,
That gentle bird, whom thou dost love,
And call'st by thy own daughter's name–
Sir Leoline! I saw the same
Fluttering, and uttering fearful moan,
Among the green herbs in the forest alone.
Which when I saw and when I heard,
I wonder'd what might ail the bird;
For nothing near it could I see,
Save the grass and green herbs underneath the old tree.

'And in my dream methought I went
To search out what might there be found;
And what the sweet bird's trouble meant,
That thus lay fluttering on the ground.
I went and peered, and could descry
No cause for her distressful cry;
But yet for her dear lady's sake

I stooped, methought, the dove to take,
When lo! I saw a bright green snake
Coiled around its wings and neck.
Green as the herbs on which it couched,
Close by the dove's its head it crouched;
And with the dove it heaves and stirs,
Swelling its neck as she swelled hers!
I woke; it was the midnight hour,
The clock was echoing in the tower;
But though my slumber was gone by,
This dream it would not pass away–
It seems to live upon my eye!
And thence I vowed this self-same day
With music strong and saintly song
To wander through the forest bare,
Lest aught unholy loiter there.'

Thus Bracy said: the Baron, the while,
Half-listening heard him with a smile;
Then turned to Lady Geraldine,
His eyes made up of wonder and love;
And said in courtly accents fine,
'Sweet maid, Lord Roland's beauteous dove,
With arms more strong than harp or song,
Thy sire and I will crush the snake!'
He kissed her forehead as he spake,
And Geraldine in maiden wise
Casting down her large bright eyes,
With blushing cheek and courtesy fine
She turned her from Sir Leoline;
Softly gathering up her train,
That o'er her right arm fell again;
And folded her arms across her chest,
And couched her head upon her breast,

And looked askance at Christabel–
Jesu, Maria, shield her well!

A snake's small eye blinks dull and shy;
And the lady's eyes they shrunk in her head,
Each shrunk up to a serpent's eye,
And with somewhat of malice, and more of dread,
At Christabel she looked askance!–
One moment–and the sight was fled!
But Christabel in dizzy trance
Stumbling on the unsteady ground
Shuddered aloud, with a hissing sound;
And Geraldine again turned round,
And like a thing, that sought relief,
Full of wonder and full of grief,
She rolled her large bright eyes divine
Wildly on Sir Leoline.

The maid, alas! her thoughts are gone,
She nothing sees–no sight but one!
The maid, devoid of guile and sin,
I know not how, in fearful wise,
So deeply had she drunken in
That look, those shrunken serpent eyes,
That all her features were resigned
To this sole image in her mind:
And passively did imitate
That look of dull and treacherous hate!
And thus she stood, in dizzy trance,
Still picturing that look askance
With forced unconscious sympathy
Full before her father's view––
As far as such a look could be
In eyes so innocent and blue!

And when the trance was o'er, the maid
Paused awhile, and inly prayed:
Then falling at the Baron's feet,
'By my mother's soul do I entreat
That thou this woman send away!'
She said: and more she could not say:
For what she knew she could not tell,
O'er-mastered by the mighty spell.

Why is thy cheek so wan and wild,
Sir Leoline? Thy only child
Lies at thy feet, thy joy, thy pride,
So fair, so innocent, so mild;
The same, for whom thy lady died!
O by the pangs of her dear mother
Think thou no evil of thy child!
For her, and thee, and for no other,
She prayed the moment ere she died:
Prayed that the babe for whom she died,
Might prove her dear lord's joy and pride!
  That prayer her deadly pangs beguiled,
    Sir Leoline!
  And wouldst thou wrong thy only child,
    Her child and thine?

Within the Baron's heart and brain
If thoughts, like these, had any share,
They only swelled his rage and pain,
And did but work confusion there.
His heart was cleft with pain and rage,
His cheeks they quivered, his eyes were wild,
Dishonoured thus in his old age;
Dishonoured by his only child,
And all his hospitality

To the wronged daughter of his friend
By more than woman's jealousy
Brought thus to a disgraceful end–
He rolled his eye with stern regard
Upon the gentle minstrel bard,
And said in tones abrupt, austere–
'Why, Bracy! dost thou loiter here?
I bade thee hence!' The bard obeyed;
And turning from his own sweet maid,
The agéd knight, Sir Leoline,
Led forth the lady Geraldine!

1800.

The Conclusion to Part II

A little child, a limber elf,
Singing, dancing to itself,
A fairy thing with red round cheeks,
That always finds, and never seeks,
Makes such a vision to the sight
As fills a father's eyes with light;
And pleasures flow in so thick and fast
Upon his heart, that he at last
Must needs express his love's excess
With words of unmeant bitterness.
Perhap 'tis pretty to force together
Thoughts so all unlike each other;
To mutter and mock a broken charm,
To dally with wrong that does no harm.
Perhaps 'tis tender too and pretty
At each wild word to feel within
A sweet recoil of love and pity.

And what, if in a world of sin
(O sorrow and shame should this be true!)
Such giddiness of heart and brain
Comes seldom save from rage and pain,
So talks as it's most used to do.

1801.

KUBLA KHAN

In Xanadu did Kubla Khan
A stately pleasure-dome decree:
Where Alph, the sacred river, ran
Through caverns measureless to man
   Down to a sunless sea.
So twice five miles of fertile ground
With walls and towers were girdled round:
And there were gardens bright with sinuous rills,
Where blossomed many an incense-bearing tree;
And here were forests ancient as the hills,
Enfolding sunny spots of greenery.

But oh! that deep romantic chasm which slanted
Down the green hill athwart a cedarn cover!
A savage place! as holy and enchanted
As e'er beneath a waning moon was haunted
By woman wailing for her demon-lover!
And from this chasm, with ceaseless turmoil seething,
As if this earth in fast thick pants were breathing,
A mighty fountain momently was forced:
Amid whose swift half-intermitted burst
Huge fragments vaulted like rebounding hail,

Or chaffy grain beneath the thresher's flail:
And 'mid these dancing rocks at once and ever
It flung up momently the sacred river.
Five miles meandering with a mazy motion
Through wood and dale the sacred river ran,
Then reached the caverns measureless to man,
And sank in tumult to a lifeless ocean:
And 'mid this tumult Kubla heard from far
Ancestral voices prophesying war!

The shadow of the dome of pleasure
Floated midway on the waves;
Where was heard the mingled measure
From the fountain and the caves.
It was a miracle of rare device,
A sunny pleasure-dome with caves of ice!

A damsel with a dulcimer
In a vision once I saw:
It was an Abyssinian maid,
And on her dulcimer she played,
Singing of Mount Abora.
Could I revive within me
Her symphony and song,
To such a deep delight 'twould win me,
That with music loud and long,
would build that dome in air,
That sunny dome! those caves of ice!
And all who heard should see them there,
And all should cry, Beware! Beware!
His flashing eyes, his floating hair!
Weave a circle round him thrice,
And close your eyes with holy dread,
For he on honey-dew hath fed,
And drunk the milk of Paradise.

1798.

PART 2:

CONVERSATION POEMS

THE EOLIAN HARP

COMPOSED AT CLEVEDON, SOMERSETSHIRE

My pensive Sara! thy soft cheek reclined
Thus on mine arm, most soothing sweet it is
To sit beside our Cot, our Cot o'ergrown
With white-flower'd Jasmin, and the broad-leav'd Myrtle,
(Meet emblems they of Innocence and Love!)
And watch the clouds, that late were rich with light.
Slow saddening round, and mark the star of eve
Serenely brilliant (such should Wisdom be)
Shine opposite! How exquisite the scents
Snatch'd from yon bean-field! and the world *so* hush'd!
The stilly murmur of the distant Sea
Tells us of silence.

And that simplest Lute,
Placed length-ways in the clasping casement, hark!
How by the desultory breeze caress'd,
Like some coy maid half yielding to her lover,
It pours such sweet upbraiding, as must needs
Tempt to repeat the wrong! And now, its strings
Boldlier swept, the long sequacious notes
Over delicious surges sink and rise,
Such a soft floating witchery of sound

As twilight Elfins make, when they at eve
Voyage on gentle gales from Fairy-Land,
Where Melodies round honey-dropping flowers,
Footless and wild, like birds of Paradise,
Nor pause, nor perch, hovering on untam'd wing!
O! the one Life within us and abroad,
Which meets all motion and becomes its soul,
A light in sound, a sound-like power in light,
Rhythm in all thought, and joyance every where–
Methinks, it should have been impossible
Not to love all things in a world so fill'd;
Where the breeze warbles, and the mute still air
Is Music slumbering on her instrument.

And thus, my Love! as on the midway slope
Of yonder hill I stretch my limbs at noon,
Whilst through my half-closed eye-lids I behold
The sunbeams dance, like diamonds, on the main,
And tranquil muse upon tranquillity;
Full many a thought uncall'd and undetain'd,
And many idle flitting phantasies,
Traverse my indolent and passive brain,
As wild and various as the random gales
That swell and flutter on this subject Lute!

And what if all of animated nature
Be but organic Harps diversely fram'd,
That tremble into thought, as o'er them sweeps
Plastic and vast, one intellectual breeze,
At once the Soul of each, and God of all?

But thy more serious eye a mild reproof
Darts, O belovéd Woman! nor such thoughts
Dim and unhallow'd dost thou not reject,
And biddest me walk humbly with my God.

Meek Daughter in the family of Christ!
Well hast thou said and holily disprais'd
These shapings of the unregenerate mind;
Bubbles that glitter as they rise and break
On vain Philosophy's aye-babbling spring.
For never guiltless may I speak of him,
The Incomprehensible! save when with awe
I praise him, and with Faith that inly *feels*;
Who with his saving mercies healéd me,
A sinful and most miserable man,
Wilder'd and dark, and gave me to possess
Peace, and this Cot, and thee, heart-honour'd Maid!

1795.

REFLECTIONS ON HAVING LEFT A PLACE OF RETIREMENT

Low was our pretty Cot: our tallest Rose
Peep'd at the chamber-window. We could hear
At silent noon, and eve, and early morn,
The Sea's faint murmur. In the open air
Our Myrtles blossom'd; and across the porch
Thick Jasmins twined: the little landscape round
Was green and woody, and refresh'd the eye.
It was a spot which you might aptly call
The Valley of Seclusion! Once I saw
(Hallowing his Sabbath-day by quietness)
A wealthy son of Commerce saunter by,
Bristowa's citizen: methought, it calm'd
His thirst of idle gold, and made him muse
With wiser feelings: for he paus'd, and look'd
With a pleas'd sadness, and gaz'd all around,
Then eyed our Cottage, and gaz'd round again,
And sigh'd, and said, it was a Blessèd Place.
And we *were* bless'd. Oft with patient ear
Long-listening to the viewless sky-lark's note
(Viewless, or haply for a moment seen
Gleaming on sunny wings) in whisper'd tones

I've said to my Belovèd, 'Such, sweet Girl!
The inobtrusive song of Happiness,
Unearthly minstrelsy! then only heard
When the Soul seeks to hear; when all is hush'd,
And the Heart listens!'

But the time, when first
From that low Dell, steep up the stony Mount
I climb'd with perilous toil and reach'd the top,
Oh! what a goodly scene! *Here* the bleak mount,
The bare bleak mountain speckled thin with sheep;
Grey clouds, that shadowing spot the sunny fields;
And river, now with bushy rocks o'er-brow'd,
Now winding bright and full, with naked banks;
And seats, and lawns, the Abbey and the wood,
And cots, and hamlets, and faint city-spire;
The Channel *there*, the Islands and white sails,
Dim coasts, and cloud-like hills, and shoreless Ocean–
It seem'd like Omnipresence! God, methought,
Had built him there a Temple: the whole World
Seem'd *imag'd* in its vast circumference:
No *wish* profan'd my overwhelméd heart.
Blest hour! It was a luxury,–to be!

Ah! quiet Dell! dear Cot, and Mount sublime!
I was constrain'd to quit you. Was it right,
While my unnumber'd brethren toil'd and bled,
That I should dream away the entrusted hours
On rose-leaf beds, pampering the coward heart
With feelings all too delicate for use?
Sweet is the tear that from some Howard's eye
Drops on the cheek of one he lifts from earth:
And he that works me good with unmov'd face,
Does it but half: he chills me while he aids,
My benefactor, not my brother man!

Yet even this, this cold beneficence
Praise, praise it, O my Soul! oft as thou scann'st
The sluggard Pity's vision-weaving tribe!
Who sigh for Wretchedness, yet shun the Wretched,
Nursing in some delicious solitude
Their slothful loves and dainty sympathies!
I therefore go, and join head, heart, and hand,
Active and firm, to fight the bloodless fight
Of Science, Freedom, and the Truth in Christ.

Yet oft when after honourable toil
Bests the tir'd mind, and waking loves to dream,
My spirit shall revisit thee, dear Cot!
Thy Jasmin and thy window-peeping Rose,
And Myrtles fearless of the mild sea-air.
And I shall sigh fond wishes–sweet Abode!
Ah!–had none greater! And that all had such!
It might be so–but the time is not yet.
Speed it, O Father! Let thy Kingdom come!

1795.

THIS LIME-TREE BOWER MY PRISON

[ADDRESSED TO CHARLES LAMB, OF THE INDIA HOUSE, LONDON]

In the June of 1797 some long-expected friends paid a visit to the author's cottage; and on the morning of their arrival, he met with an accident, which disabled him from walking during the whole time of their stay. One evening, when they had left him for a few hours, he composed the following lines in the garden-bower.

Well, they are gone, and here must I remain,
This lime-tree bower my prison! I have lost
Beauties and feelings, such as would have been
Most sweet to my remembrance even when age
Had dimm'd mine eyes to blindness! They, meanwhile,
Friends, whom I never more may meet again,
On springy heath, along the hill-top edge,
Wander in gladness, and wind down, perchance,
To that still roaring dell, of which I told;
The roaring dell, o'erwooded, narrow, deep,
And only speckled by the mid-day sun;
Where its slim trunk the ash from rock to rock
Flings arching like a bridge;—that branchless ash,

Unsunn'd and damp, whose few poor yellow leaves
Ne'er tremble in the gale, yet tremble still,
Fann'd by the water-fall! and there my friends
Behold the dark green file of long lank weeds,
That all at once (a most fantastic sight!)
Still nod and drip beneath the dripping edge
Of the blue clay-stone.

Now, my friends emerge
Beneath the wide wide Heaven–and view again
The many-steepled tract magnificent
Of hilly fields and meadows, and the sea,
With some fair bark, perhaps, whose sails light up
The slip of smooth clear blue betwixt two Isles
Of purple shadow! Yes! they wander on
In gladness all; but thou, methinks, most glad,
My gentle-hearted Charles! for thou hast pined
And hunger'd after Nature, many a year,
In the great City pent, winning thy way
With sad yet patient soul, through evil and pain
And strange calamity! Ah! slowly sink
Behind the western ridge, thou glorious Sun!
Shine in the slant beams of the sinking orb,
Ye purple heath-flowers! richlier burn, ye clouds!
Live in the yellow light, ye distant groves!
And kindle, thou blue Ocean! So my friend
Struck with deep joy may stand, as I have stood,
Silent with swimming sense; yea, gazing round
On the wide landscape, gaze till all doth seem
Less gross than bodily; and of such hues
As veil the Almighty Spirit, when yet he makes
Spirits perceive his presence.

A delight
Comes sudden on my heart, and I am glad
As I myself were there! Nor in this bower,
This little lime-tree bower, have I not mark'd
Much that has sooth'd me. Pale beneath the blaze
Hung the transparent foliage; and I watch'd
Some broad and sunny leaf, and lov'd to see
The shadow of the leaf and stem above
Dappling its sunshine! And that walnut-tree
Was richly ting'd, and a deep radiance lay
Full on the ancient ivy, which usurps
Those fronting elms, and now, with blackest mass
Makes their dark branches gleam a lighter hue
Through the late twilight: and though now the bat
Wheels silent by, and not a swallow twitters,
Yet still the solitary humble-bee
Sings in the bean-flower! Henceforth I shall know
That Nature ne'er deserts the wise and pure;
No plot so narrow, be but Nature there,
No waste so vacant, but may well employ
Each faculty of sense, and keep the heart
Awake to Love and Beauty! and sometimes
'Tis well to be bereft of promis'd good,
That we may lift the soul, and contemplate
With lively joy the joys we cannot share.
My gentle-hearted Charles! when the last rook
Beat its straight path along the dusky air
Homewards, I blest it! deeming its black wing
(Now a dim speck, now vanishing in light)
Had cross'd the mighty Orb's dilated glory,
While thou stood'st gazing; or, when all was still,
Flew creeking o'er thy head, and had a charm
For thee, my gentle-hearted Charles, to whom
No sound is dissonant which tells of Life.

1797.

FROST AT MIDNIGHT

The Frost performs its secret ministry,
Unhelped by any wind. The owlet's cry
Came loud–and hark, again! loud as before.
The inmates of my cottage, all at rest,
Have left me to that solitude, which suits
Abstruser musings: save that at my side
My cradled infant slumbers peacefully.
'Tis calm indeed! so calm that it disturbs
And vexes meditation with its strange
And extreme silentness. Sea, hill, and wood,
This populous village! Sea, and hill, and wood,
With all the numberless goings-on of life,
Inaudible as dreams! the thin blue flame
Lies on my low-burnt fire, and quivers not;
Only that film, which fluttered on the grate,
Still flutters there, the sole unquiet thing.
Methinks, its motion in this hush of nature
Gives it dim sympathies with me who live,
Making it a companionable form,
Whose puny flaps and freaks the idling Spirit
By its own moods interprets, every where

Echo or mirror seeking of itself,
And makes a toy of Thought.

But O! how oft,
How oft, at school, with most believing mind,
Presageful, have I gazed upon the bars,
To watch that fluttering stranger! and as oft
With unclosed lids, already had I dreamt
Of my sweet birth-place, and the old church-tower,
Whose bells, the poor man's only music, rang
From morn to evening, all the hot Fair-day,
So sweetly, that they stirred and haunted me
With a wild pleasure, falling on mine ear
Most like articulate sounds of things to come!
So gazed I, till the soothing things, I dreamt,
Lulled me to sleep, and sleep prolonged my dreams!
And so I brooded all the following morn,
Awed by the stern preceptor's face, mine eye
Fixed with mock study on my swimming book:
Save if the door half opened, and I snatched
A hasty glance, and still my heart leaped up,
For still I hoped to see the stranger's face,
Townsman, or aunt, or sister more beloved,
My play-mate when we both were clothed alike!

Dear Babe, that sleepest cradled by my side,
Whose gentle breathings, heard in this deep calm,
Fill up the interspersèd vacancies
And momentary pauses of the thought!
My babe so beautiful! it thrills my heart
With tender gladness, thus to look at thee,
And think that thou shalt learn far other lore,
And in far other scenes! For I was reared
In the great city, pent 'mid cloisters dim,
And saw nought lovely but the sky and stars.

But *thou*, my babe! shalt wander like a breeze
By lakes and sandy shores, beneath the crags
Of ancient mountain, and beneath the clouds,
Which image in their bulk both lakes and shores
And mountain crags: so shalt thou see and hear
The lovely shapes and sounds intelligible
Of that eternal language, which thy God
Utters, who from eternity doth teach
Himself in all, and all things in himself.
Great universal Teacher! he shall mould
Thy spirit, and by giving make it ask.

Therefore all seasons shall be sweet to thee,
Whether the summer clothe the general earth
With greenness, or the redbreast sit and sing
Betwixt the tufts of snow on the bare branch
Of mossy apple-tree, while the nigh thatch
Smokes in the sun-thaw; whether the eave-drops fall
Heard only in the trances of the blast,
Or if the secret ministry of frost
Shall hang them up in silent icicles,
Quietly shining to the quiet Moon.

February, 1798.

FEARS IN SOLITUDE

WRITTEN IN APRIL 1798, DURING THE ALARM OF AN INVASION

A green and silent spot, amid the hills,
A small and silent dell! O'er stiller place
No singing sky-lark ever poised himself.
The hills are heathy, save that swelling slope,
Which hath a gay and gorgeous covering on,
All golden with the never-bloomless furze,
Which now blooms most profusely: but the dell,
Bathed by the mist, is fresh and delicate
As vernal corn-field, or the unripe flax,
When, through its half-transparent stalks, at eve,
The level sunshine glimmers with green light.
Oh! 'tis a quiet spirit-healing nook!
Which all, methinks, would love; but chiefly he,
The humble man, who, in his youthful years,
Knew just so much of folly, as had made
His early manhood more securely wise!
Here he might lie on fern or withered heath,
While from the singing lark (that sings unseen
The minstrelsy that solitude loves best),
And from the sun, and from the breezy air,
Sweet influences trembled o'er his frame;
And he, with many feelings, many thoughts,

Made up a meditative joy, and found
Religious meanings in the forms of Nature!
And so, his senses gradually wrapt
In a half sleep, he dreams of better worlds,
And dreaming hears thee still, O singing lark,
That singest like an angel in the clouds!

My God! it is a melancholy thing
For such a man, who would full fain preserve
His soul in calmness, yet perforce must feel
For all his human brethren–O my God!
It weighs upon the heart, that he must think
What uproar and what strife may now be stirring
This way or that way o'er these silent hills–
Invasion, and the thunder and the shout,
And all the crash of onset; fear and rage,
And undetermined conflict–even now,
Even now, perchance, and in his native isle:
Carnage and groans beneath this blessed sun!
We have offended, Oh! my countrymen!
We have offended very grievously,
And been most tyrannous. From east to west
A groan of accusation pierces Heaven!
The wretched plead against us; multitudes
Countless and vehement, the sons of God,
Our brethren! Like a cloud that travels on.
Steamed up from Cairo's swamps of pestilence,
Even so, my countrymen! have we gone forth
And borne to distant tribes slavery and pangs,
And, deadlier far, our vices, whose deep taint
With slow perdition murders the whole man,
His body and his soul! Meanwhile, at home,
All individual dignity and power
Engulfed in Courts, Committees, Institutions,
Associations and Societies,

A vain, speech-mouthing, speech-reporting Guild,
One Benefit-Club for mutual flattery,
We have drunk up, demure as at a grace,
Pollutions from the brimming cup of wealth;
Contemptuous of all honourable rule,
Yet bartering freedom and the poor man's life
For gold, as at a market! The sweet words
Of Christian promise, words that even yet
Might stem destruction, were they wisely preached,
Are muttered o'er by men, whose tones proclaim
How flat and wearisome they feel their trade:
Rank scoffers some, but most too indolent
To deem them falsehoods or to know their truth.
Oh! blasphemous! the Book of Life is made
A superstitious instrument, on which
We gabble o'er the oaths we mean to break;
For all must swear–all and in every place,
College and wharf, council and justice-court;
All, all must swear, the briber and the bribed,
Merchant and lawyer, senator and priest,
The rich, the poor, the old man and the young;
All, all make up one scheme of perjury,
That faith doth reel; the very name of God
Sounds like a juggler's charm; and, bold with joy,
Forth from his dark and lonely hiding-place,
(Portentous sight!) the owlet Atheism,
Sailing on obscene wings athwart the noon,
Drops his blue-fringed lids, and holds them close,
And hooting at the glorious sun in Heaven,
Cries out, 'Where is it?'

Thankless too for peace,
(Peace long preserved by fleets and perilous seas)
Secure from actual warfare, we have loved
To swell the war-whoop, passionate for war!

Alas! for ages ignorant of all
Its ghastlier workings, (famine or blue plague,
Battle, or siege, or flight through wintry snows,)
We, this whole people, have been clamorous
For war and bloodshed; animating sports,
The which we pay for as a thing to talk of,
Spectators and not combatants! No guess
Anticipative of a wrong unfelt,
No speculation on contingency,
However dim and vague, too vague and dim
To yield a justifying cause; and forth,
(Stuffed out with big preamble, holy names.
And adjurations of the God in Heaven.)
We send our mandates for the certain death
Of thousands and ten thousands! Boys and girls,
And women, that would groan to see a child
Pull off an insect's leg, all read of war,
The best amusement for our morning meal!
The poor wretch, who has learnt his only prayers
From curses, who knows scarcely words enough
To ask a blessing from his Heavenly Father,
Becomes a fluent phraseman, absolute
And technical in victories and defeats,
And all our dainty terms for fratricide;
Terms which we trundle smoothly o'er our tongues
Like mere abstractions, empty sounds to which
We join no feeling and attach no form!
As if the soldier died without a wound;
As if the fibres of this godlike frame
Were gored without a pang; as if the wretch,
Who fell in battle, doing bloody deeds,
Passed off to Heaven, translated and not killed;
As though he had no wife to pine for him,
No God to judge him! Therefore, evil days
Are coming on us, O my countrymen!

And what if all-avenging Providence,
Strong and retributive, should make us know
The meaning of our words, force us to feel
The desolation and the agony
Of our fierce doings?

Spare us yet awhile,
Father and God! O! spare us yet awhile!
Oh! let not English women drag their flight
Fainting beneath the burthen of their babes,
Of the sweet infants, that but yesterday
Laughed at the breast! Sons, brothers, husbands, all
Who ever gazed with fondness on the forms
Which grew up with you round the same fire-side,
And all who ever heard the sabbath-bells
Without the infidel's scorn, make yourselves pure!
Stand forth! be men! repel an impious foe,
Impious and false, a light yet cruel race,
Who laugh away all virtue, mingling mirth
With deeds of murder; and still promising
Freedom, themselves too sensual to be free,
Poison life's amities, and cheat the heart
Of faith and quiet hope, and all that soothes,
And all that lifts the spirit! Stand we forth;
Render them back upon the insulted ocean,
And let them toss as idly on its waves
As the vile sea-weed, which some mountain-blast
Swept from our shores! And oh! may we return
Not with a drunken triumph, but with fear,
Repenting of the wrongs with which we stung
So fierce a foe to frenzy!

I have told,
O Britons! O my brethren! I have told
Most bitter truth, but without bitterness.

Nor deem my zeal or factious or mistimed;
For never can true courage dwell with them,
Who, playing tricks with conscience, dare not look
At their own vices. We have been too long
Dupes of a deep delusion! Some, belike,
Groaning with restless enmity, expect
All change from change of constituted power;
As if a Government had been a robe,
On which our vice and wretchedness were tagged
Like fancy-points and fringes, with the robe
Pulled off at pleasure. Fondly these attach
A radical causation to a few
Poor drudges of chastising Providence,
Who borrow all their hues and qualities
From our own folly and rank wickedness,
Which gave them birth and nursed them. Others,
meanwhile,
Dote with a mad idolatry; and all
Who will not fall before their images,
And yield them worship, they are enemies
Even of their country!

Such have I been deemed.–
But, O dear Britain! O my Mother Isle!
Needs must thou prove a name most dear and holy
To me, a son, a brother, and a friend,
A husband, and a father! who revere
All bonds of natural love, and find them all
Within the limits of thy rocky shores.
O native Britain! O my Mother Isle!
How shouldst thou prove aught else but dear and holy
To me, who from thy lakes and mountain-hills,
Thy clouds, thy quiet dales, thy rocks and seas,
Have drunk in all my intellectual life,
All sweet sensations, all ennobling thoughts,

All adoration of the God in nature,
All lovely and all honourable things.
Whatever makes this mortal spirit feel
The joy and greatness of its future being?
There lives nor form nor feeling in my soul
Unborrowed from my country! O divine
And beauteous island! thou hast been my sole
And most magnificent temple, in the which
I walk with awe, and sing my stately songs,
Loving the God that made me!–

May my fears,
My filial fears, be vain! and may the vaunts
And menace of the vengeful enemy
Pass like the gust, that roared and died away
In the distant tree: which heard, and only heard
In this low dell, bowed not the delicate grass.

But now the gentle dew-fall sends abroad
The fruit-like perfume of the golden furze:
The light has left the summit of the hill,
Though still a sunny gleam lies beautiful,
Aslant the ivied beacon. Now farewell,
Farewell, awhile, O soft and silent spot!
On the green sheep-track, up the heathy hill,
Homeward I wind my way; and lo! recalled
From bodings that have well-nigh wearied me,
I find myself upon the brow, and pause
Startled! And after lonely sojourning
In such a quiet and surrounded nook,
This burst of prospect, here the shadowy main,
Dim-tinted, there the mighty majesty
Of that huge amphitheatre of rich
And elmy fields, seems like society–
Conversing with the mind, and giving it

A livelier impulse and a dance of thought!
And now, beloved Stowey! I behold
Thy church-tower, and, methinks, the four huge elms
Clustering, which mark the mansion of my friend;
And close behind them, hidden from my view,
Is my own lowly cottage, where my babe
And my babe's mother dwell in peace! With light
And quickened footsteps thitherward I tend,
Remembering thee, O green and silent dell!
And grateful, that by nature's quietness
And solitary musings, all my heart
Is softened, and made worthy to indulge
Love, and the thoughts that yearn for human kind.

Nether Stowey, April 20, 1798.

THE NIGHTINGALE

A CONVERSATION POEM, APRIL, 1798

No cloud, no relique of the sunken day
Distinguishes the West, no long thin slip
Of sullen light, no obscure trembling hues.
Come, we will rest on this old mossy bridge!
You see the glimmer of the stream beneath,
But hear no murmuring: it flows silently,
O'er its soft bed of verdure. All is still,
A balmy night! and though the stars be dim,
Yet let us think upon the vernal showers
That gladden the green earth, and we shall find
A pleasure in the dimness of the stars.
And hark! the Nightingale begins its song,
'Most musical, most melancholy' bird!
A melancholy bird? Oh! idle thought!
In Nature there is nothing melancholy.
But some night-wandering man whose heart was pierced
With the remembrance of a grievous wrong,
Or slow distemper, or neglected love,
(And so, poor wretch! filled all things with himself,
And made all gentle sounds tell back the tale
Of his own sorrow) he, and such as he,
First named these notes a melancholy strain.

And many a poet echoes the conceit;
Poet who hath been building up the rhyme
When he had better far have stretched his limbs
Beside a brook in mossy forest-dell,
By sun or moon-light, to the influxes
Of shapes and sounds and shifting elements
Surrendering his whole spirit, of his song
And of his fame forgetful! so his fame
Should share in Nature's immortality,
A venerable thing! and so his song
Should make all Nature lovelier, and itself
Be loved like Nature! But 'twill not be so;
And youths and maidens most poetical,
Who lose the deepening twilights of the spring
In ball-rooms and hot theatres, they still
Full of meek sympathy must heave their sighs
O'er Philomela's pity-pleading strains.

My Friend, and thou, our Sister! we have learnt
A different lore: we may not thus profane
Nature's sweet voices, always full of love
And joyance! 'Tis the merry Nightingale
That crowds, and hurries, and precipitates
With fast thick warble his delicious notes,
As he were fearful that an April night
Would be too short for him to utter forth
His love-chant, and disburthen his full soul
Of all its music!

And I know a grove
Of large extent, hard by a castle huge,
Which the great lord inhabits not; and so
This grove is wild with tangling underwood,
And the trim walks are broken up, and grass,
Thin grass and king-cups grow within the paths.

But never elsewhere in one place I knew
So many nightingales; and far and near,
In wood and thicket, over the wide grove,
They answer and provoke each other's song,
With skirmish and capricious passagings,
And murmurs musical and swift jug jug,
And one low piping sound more sweet than all–
Stirring the air with such a harmony,
That should you close your eyes, you might almost
Forget it was not day! On moonlight bushes,
Whose dewy leaflets are but half-disclosed.
You may perchance behold them on the twigs,
Their bright, bright eyes, their eyes both bright and full,
Glistening, while many a glow-worm in the shade
Lights up her love-torch.

A most gentle Maid,
Who dwelleth in her hospitable home
Hard by the castle, and at latest eve
(Even like a Lady vowed and dedicate
To something more than Nature in the grove)
Glides through the pathways; she knows all their notes,
That gentle Maid! and oft, a moment's space,
What time the moon was lost behind a cloud,
Hath heard a pause of silence; till the moon
Emerging, hath awakened earth and sky
With one sensation, and those wakeful birds
Have all burst forth in choral minstrelsy,
As if some sudden gale had swept at once
A hundred airy harps! And she hath watched
Many a nightingale perch giddily
On blossomy twig still swinging from the breeze,
And to that motion tune his wanton song
Like tipsy Joy that reels with tossing head.

Farewell, O Warbler! till to-morrow eve,
And you, my friends! farewell, a short farewell!
We have been loitering long and pleasantly,
And now for our dear homes.–That strain again!
Full fain it would delay me! My dear babe,
Who, capable of no articulate sound,
Mars all things with his imitative lisp,
How he would place his hand beside his ear,
His little hand, the small forefinger up,
And bid us listen! And I deem it wise
To make him Nature's play-mate. He knows well
The evening-star; and once, when he awoke
In most distressful mood (some inward pain
Had made up that strange thing, an infant's dream–)
I hurried with him to our orchard-plot,
And he beheld the moon, and, hushed at once,
Suspends his sobs, and laughs most silently,
While his fair eyes, that swam with undropped tears,
Did glitter in the yellow moon-beam! Well!–
It is a father's tale: But if that Heaven
Should give me life, his childhood shall grow up
Familiar with these songs, that with the night
He may associate joy.–Once more, farewell,
Sweet Nightingale! once more, my friends! farewell.

1798.

DEJECTION: AN ODE

[WRITTEN APRIL 4, 1802]

Late, late yestreen I saw the new Moon,
With the old Moon in her arms;
And I fear, I fear, my Master dear!
We shall have a deadly storm.
Ballad of Sir Patrick Spence

I

Well! If the Bard was weather-wise, who made
The grand old ballad of Sir Patrick Spence,
This night, so tranquil now, will not go hence
Unroused by winds, that ply a busier trade
Than those which mould yon cloud in lazy flakes,
Or the dull sobbing draft, that moans and rakes
Upon the strings of this Æolian lute,
Which better far were mute.
For lo! the New-moon winter-bright!
And overspread with phantom light,
(With swimming phantom light o'erspread
But rimmed and circled by a silver thread)
I see the old Moon in her lap, foretelling

The coming-on of rain and squally blast.
And oh! that even now the gust were swelling,
And the slant night-shower driving loud and fast!
Those sounds which oft have raised me, whilst they awed,
And sent my soul abroad,
Might now perhaps their wonted impulse give,
Might startle this dull pain, and make it move and live!

II

A grief without a pang, void, dark, and drear,
A stifled, drowsy, unimpassioned grief,
Which finds no natural outlet, no relief,
In word, or sigh, or tear–
O Lady! in this wan and heartless mood,
To other thoughts by yonder throstle woo'd,
All this long eve, so balmy and serene,
Have I been gazing on the western sky,
And its peculiar tint of yellow green:
And still I gaze–and with how blank an eye!
And those thin clouds above, in flakes and bars,
That give away their motion to the stars;
Those stars, that glide behind them or between,
Now sparkling, now bedimmed, but always seen:
Yon crescent Moon, as fixed as if it grew
In its own cloudless, starless lake of blue;
I see them all so excellently fair,
I see, not feel, how beautiful they are!

III

My genial spirits fail;
And what can these avail

To lift the smothering weight from off my breast?
    It were a vain endeavour,
    Though I should gaze for ever
On that green light that lingers in the west:
I may not hope from outward forms to win
The passion and the Life, whose fountains are within.

IV

O Lady! we receive but what we give,
And in our life alone does Nature live:
Ours is her wedding garment, ours her shroud!
   And would we aught behold, of higher worth,
Than that inanimate cold world allowed
To the poor loveless ever-anxious crowd,
   Ah! from the soul itself must issue forth
A light, a glory, a fair luminous cloud
    Enveloping the Earth–
And from the soul itself must there be sent
   A sweet and potent voice, of its own birth,
Of all sweet sounds the life and element!

V

O pure of heart! thou need'st not ask of me
What this strong music in the soul may be!
What, and wherein it doth exist,
This light, this glory, this fair luminous mist,
This beautiful and beauty-making power.
   Joy, virtuous Lady! Joy that ne'er was given,
Save to the pure, and in their purest hour,
Life, and Life's effluence, cloud at once and shower,
Joy, Lady! is the spirit and the power,

Which wedding Nature to us gives in dower
  A new Earth and new Heaven,
Undreamt of by the sensual and the proud–
Joy is the sweet voice, Joy the luminous cloud–
    We in ourselves rejoice!
And thence flows all that charms or ear or sight,
  All melodies the echoes of that voice,
All colours a suffusion from that light.

VI

There was a time when, though my path was rough,
  This joy within me dallied with distress,
And all misfortunes were but as the stuff
  Whence Fancy made me dreams of happiness:
For hope grew round me, like the twining vine,
And fruits, and foliage, not my own, seemed mine.
But now afflictions bow me down to earth:
Nor care I that they rob me of my mirth;
    But oh! each visitation
Suspends what nature gave me at my birth,
  My shaping spirit of Imagination.
For not to think of what I needs must feel,
  But to be still and patient, all I can;
And haply by abstruse research to steal
  From my own nature all the natural man–
  This was my sole resource, my only plan:
Till that which suits a part infects the whole,
And now is almost grown the habit of my soul.

VII

Hence, viper thoughts, that coil around my mind,
Reality's dark dream!
I turn from you, and listen to the wind,
Which long has raved unnoticed. What a scream
Of agony by torture lengthened out
That lute sent forth! Thou Wind, that rav'st without,
Bare crag, or mountain-tairn, or blasted tree,
Or pine-grove whither woodman never clomb,
Or lonely house, long held the witches' home,
Methinks were fitter instruments for thee,
Mad Lutanist! who in this month of showers,
Of dark-brown gardens, and of peeping flowers,
Mak'st Devils' yule, with worse than wintry song,
The blossoms, buds, and timorous leaves among.
Thou Actor, perfect in all tragic sounds!
Thou mighty Poet, e'en to frenzy bold!
What tell'st thou now about?
'Tis of the rushing of an host in rout,
With groans, of trampled men, with smarting wounds–
At once they groan with pain, and shudder with the
cold!
But hush! there is a pause of deepest silence!
And all that noise, as of a rushing crowd,
With groans, and tremulous shudderings–all is over–
It tells another tale, with sounds less deep and loud!
A tale, of less affright,
And tempered with delight,
As Otway's self had framed the tender lay,–
'Tis of a little child
Upon a lonesome wild,
Not far from home, but she hath lost her way:
And now moans low in bitter grief and fear,

And now screams loud, and hopes to make
  her mother hear.

VIII

'Tis midnight, but small thoughts have I of sleep:
Full seldom may my friend such vigils keep!
Visit her, gentle Sleep! with wings of healing,
  And may this storm be but a mountain-birth,
May all the stars hang bright above her dwelling,
  Silent as though they watched the sleeping Earth!
    With light heart may she rise,
    Gay fancy, cheerful eyes,
  Joy lift her spirit, joy attune her voice;
To her may all things live, from pole to pole,
Their life the eddying of her living soul!
  O simple spirit, guided from above,
Dear Lady! friend devoutest of my choice,
Thus mayest thou ever, evermore rejoice.

1802.

TO WILLIAM WORDSWORTH

COMPOSED ON THE NIGHT AFTER HIS RECITATION OF A POEM ON THE GROWTH OF AN INDIVIDUAL MIND

Friend of the wise! and Teacher of the Good!
Into my heart have I received that Lay
More than historic, that prophetic Lay
Wherein (high theme by thee first sung aright)
Of the foundations and the building up
Of a Human Spirit thou hast dared to tell
What may be told, to the understanding mind
Revealable; and what within the mind
By vital breathings secret as the soul
Of vernal growth, oft quickens in the heart
Thoughts all too deep for words!–

Theme hard as high!
Of smiles spontaneous, and mysterious fears
(The first-born they of Reason and twin-birth),
Of tides obedient to external force,
And currents self-determined, as might seem,
Or by some inner Power; of moments awful,
Now in thy inner life, and now abroad,
When power streamed from thee, and thy soul received

The light reflected, as a light bestowed–
Of fancies fair, and milder hours of youth,
Hyblean murmurs of poetic thought
Industrious in its joy, in vales and glens
Native or outland, lakes and famous hills!
Or on the lonely high-road, when the stars
Were rising; or by secret mountain-streams,
The guides and the companions of thy way!

Of more than Fancy, of the Social Sense
Distending wide, and man beloved as man,
Where France in all her towns lay vibrating
Like some becalméd bark beneath the burst
Of Heaven's immediate thunder, when no cloud
Is visible, or shadow on the main.
For thou wert there, thine own brows garlanded,
Amid the tremor of a realm aglow,
Amid a mighty nation jubilant,
When from the general heart of human kind
Hope sprang forth like a full-born Deity!
–Of that dear Hope afflicted and struck down,
So summoned homeward, thence forth calm and sure
From the dread watch-tower of man's absolute self,
With light unwaning on her eyes, to look
Far on–herself a glory to behold,
The Angel of the vision! Then (last strain)
Of Duty, chosen Laws controlling choice,
Action and joy!–An Orphic song indeed,
A song divine of high and passionate thoughts
To their own music chaunted!

O great Bard!
Ere yet that last strain dying awed the air,
With stedfast eye I viewed thee in the choir

Of ever-enduring men. The truly great
Have all one age, and from one visible space
Shed influence! They, both in power and act,
Are permanent, and Time is not with them,
Save as it worketh for them, they in it.
Nor less a sacred Roll, than those of old,
And to be placed, as they, with gradual fame
Among the archives of mankind, thy work
Makes audible a linkéd lay of Truth,
Of Truth profound a sweet continuous lay,
Not learnt, but native, her own natural notes!
Ah! as I listened with a heart forlorn,
The pulses of my being beat anew:
And even as Life returns upon the drowned,
Life's joy rekindling roused a throng of pains–
Keen pangs of Love, awakening as a babe
Turbulent, with an outcry in the heart;
And fears self-willed, that shunned the eye of Hope;
And Hope that scarce would know itself from Fear;
Sense of past Youth, and Manhood come in vain,
And Genius given, and Knowledge won in vain;
And all which I had culled in wood-walks wild,
And all which patient toil had reared, and all,
Commune with thee had opened out–but flowers
Strewed on my corse, and borne upon my bier,
In the same coffin, for the self-same grave!

That way no more! and ill beseems it me,
Who came a welcomer in herald's guise,
Singing of Glory, and Futurity,
To wander back on such unhealthful road,
Plucking the poisons of self-harm! And ill

Such intertwine beseems triumphal wreaths
Strew'd before thy advancing!

Nor do thou,
Sage Bard! impair the memory of that hour
Of thy communion with my nobler mind
By pity or grief, already felt too long!
Nor let my words import more blame than needs.
The tumult rose and ceased: for Peace is nigh
Where Wisdom's voice has found a listening heart.
Amid the howl of more than wintry storms,
The Halcyon hears the voice of vernal hours
Already on the wing.

Eve following eve,
Dear tranquil time, when the sweet sense of Home
Is sweetest! moments for their own sake hailed
And more desired, more precious, for thy song,
In silence listening, like a devout child,
My soul lay passive, by thy various strain
Driven as in surges now beneath the stars,
With momentary stars of my own birth,
Fair constellated foam, still darting off
Into the darkness; now a tranquil sea,
Outspread and bright, yet swelling to the moon.

And when–O Friend! my comforter and guide!
Strong in thyself, and powerful to give strength!–
Thy long sustainéd Song finally closed,
And thy deep voice had ceased–yet thou thyself
Wert still before my eyes, and round us both
That happy vision of belovéd faces–
Scarce conscious, and yet conscious of its close

I sate, my being blended in one thought
(Thought was it? or aspiration? or resolve?)
Absorbed, yet hanging still upon the sound–
And when I rose, I found myself in prayer.

January, 1807.

PART 3:

OTHER POEMS
1787-1833

EASTER HOLIDAYS

I

Hail! festal Easter that dost bring
Approach of sweetly-smiling spring,
When Nature's clad in green:
When feather'd songsters through the grove
With beasts confess the power of love
And brighten all the scene.

II

Now youths the breaking stages load
That swiftly rattling o'er the road
To Greenwich haste away:
While some with sounding oars divide
Of smoothly-flowing Thames the tide
All sing the festive lay.

III

With mirthful dance they beat the ground,
Their shouts of joy the hills resound
        And catch the jocund noise:
Without a tear, without a sigh
Their moments all in transports fly
        Till evening ends their joys.

IV

But little think their joyous hearts
Of dire Misfortune's varied smarts
        Which youthful years conceal:
Thoughtless of bitter-smiling Woe
Which all mankind are born to know
        And they themselves must feel.

V

Yet he who Wisdom's paths shall keep
And Virtue firm that scorns to weep
        At ills in Fortune's power,
Through this life's variegated scene
In raging storms or calm serene
        Shall cheerful spend the hour.

VI

While steady Virtue guides his mind
Heav'n-born Content he still shall find
That never sheds a tear:
Without respect to any tide
His hours away in bliss shall glide
Like Easter all the year.

1787.

SONNET

TO THE AUTUMNAL MOON

Mild Splendour of the various-vested Night!
  Mother of wildly-working visions! hail!
I watch thy gliding, while with watery light
  Thy weak eye glimmers through a fleecy veil;
And when thou lovest thy pale orb to shroud
  Behind the gather'd blackness lost on high;
And when thou dartest from the wind-rent cloud
  Thy placid lightning o'er thc awaken'd sky.

Ah such is Hope! as changeful and as fair!
Now dimly peering on the wistful sight;
  Now hid behind the dragon-wing'd Despair:
But soon emerging in her radiant might
  She o'er the sorrow-clouded breast of Care
Sails, like a meteor kindling in its flight.

1788.

TO THE MUSE

Tho' no bold flights to thee belong;
And tho' thy lays with conscious fear,
Shrink from Judgement's eye severe,
Yet much I thank thee, Spirit of my song!
For, lovely Muse! thy sweet employ
Exalts my soul, refines my breast,
Gives each pure pleasure keener zest,
And softens sorrow into pensive Joy.
From thee I learn'd the wish to bless,
From thee to commune with my heart;
From thee, dear Muse! the gayer part,
To laugh with pity at the crowds that press
Where Fashion flaunts her robes by Folly spun,
Whose hues gay-varying wanton in the sun.

1789.

TO THE EVENING STAR

O meek attendant of Sol's setting blaze,
  I hail, sweet star, thy chaste effulgent glow;
On thee full oft with fixéd eye I gaze
  Till I, methinks, all spirit seem to grow.
O first and fairest of the starry choir,
  O loveliest 'mid the daughters of the night,
Must not the maid I love like thee inspire
  Pure joy and *calm* Delight?

Must she not be, as is thy placid sphere
  Serenely brilliant? Whilst to gaze a while
Be all my wish 'mid Fancy's high career
  E'en till she quit this scene of earthly toil;
Then Hope perchance might fondly sigh to join
Her spirit in thy kindred orb, O Star benign!

? 1790.

TO DISAPPOINTMENT

Hence! thou fiend of gloomy sway,
  That lov'st on withering blast to ride
  O'er fond Illusion's air-built pride.
Sullen Spirit! Hence! Away!

Where Avarice lurks in sordid cell,
  Or mad Ambition builds the dream,
  Or Pleasure plots th' unholy scheme
There with Guilt and Folly dwell!

But oh! when Hope on Wisdom's wing
  Prophetic whispers pure delight,
  Be distant far thy cank'rous blight,
Demon of envenom'd sting.

Then haste thee, Nymph of balmy gales!
  Thy poet's prayer, sweet May! attend!
  Oh! place my parent and my friend
'Mid her lovely native vales.

Peace, that lists the woodlark's strains,
   Health, that breathes divinest treasures,
   Laughing Hours, and Social Pleasures
Wait my friend in Cambria's plains.

Affection there with mingled ray
   Shall pour at once the raptures high
   Of filial and maternal Joy;
Haste thee then, delightful May!

And oh! may Spring's fair flowerets fade,
   May Summer cease her limbs to lave
   In cooling stream, may Autumn grave
Yellow o'er the corn-cloath'd glade;

Ere, from sweet retirement torn,
   She seek again the crowded mart:
   Nor thou, my selfish, selfish heart
Dare her slow return to mourn!

1792.

THE ROSE

As late each flower that sweetest blows
I pluck'd, the Garden's pride!
Within the petals of a Rose
A sleeping Love I spied.

Around his brows a beamy wreath
Of many a lucent hue;
All purple glow'd his cheek, beneath,
Inebriate with dew.

I softly seiz'd the unguarded Power,
Nor scared his balmy rest:
And placed him, caged within the flower,
On spotless Sara's breast.

But when unweeting of the guile
Awoke the prisoner sweet,
He struggled to escape awhile
And stamp'd his faery feet.

Ah! soon the soul-entrancing sight
Subdued the impatient boy!
He gazed! he thrill'd with deep delight!
Then clapp'd his wings for joy.

'And O!' he cried–'Of magic kind
What charms this Throne endear!
Some other Love let Venus find–
I'll fix *my* empire *here*.'

1793.

THE HOUR WHEN WE SHALL MEET AGAIN

(COMPOSED DURING ILLNESS, AND IN ABSENCE.)

Dim Hour! that sleep'st on pillowing clouds afar,
O rise and yoke the Turtles to thy car!
Bend o'er the traces, blame each lingering Dove,
And give me to the bosom of my Love!
My gentle Love, caressing and carest,
With heaving heart shall cradle me to rest!
Shed the warm tear-drop from her smiling eyes,
Lull with fond woe, and medicine me with sighs!
While finely-flushing float her kisses meek,
Like melted rubies, o'er my pallid cheek.
Chill'd by the night, the drooping Rose of May
Mourns the long absence of the lovely Day;
Young Day returning at her promis'd hour
Weeps o'er the sorrows of her favourite Flower;
Weeps the soft dew, the balmy gale she sighs,
And darts a trembling lustre from her eyes.
New life and joy th' expanding flow'ret feels:
His pitying Mistress mourns, and mourning heals!

? 1795.

THE RAVEN

A CHRISTMAS TALE, TOLD BY A SCHOOL-BOY TO HIS LITTLE BROTHERS AND SISTERS

Underneath an old oak tree
There was of swine a huge company,
That grunted as they crunched the mast:
For that was ripe, and fell full fast.
Then they trotted away, for the wind grew high:
One acorn they left, and no more might you spy.
Next came a Raven, that liked not such folly:
He belonged, they did say, to the witch Melancholy!
Blacker was he than blackest jet,
Flew low in the rain, and his feathers not wet.
He picked up the acorn and buried it straight
By the side of a river both deep and great.
    Where then did the Raven go?
    He went high and low,
Over hill, over dale, did the black Raven go.
    Many Autumns, many Springs
    Travelled he with wandering wings:
    Many Summers, many Winters–
    I can't tell half his adventures.

At length he came back, and with him a She,
And the acorn was grown to a tall oak tree.
They built them a nest in the topmost bough,
And young ones they had, and were happy enow.
But soon came a Woodman in leathern guise,
His brow, like a pent-house, hung over his eyes.
He'd an axe in his hand, not a word he spoke,
But with many a hem! and a sturdy stroke,
At length he brought down the poor Raven's own oak.
His young ones were killed; for they could not depart,
And their mother did die of a broken heart.
The boughs from the trunk the Woodman did sever;
And they floated it down on the course of the river.
They sawed it in planks, and its bark they did strip,
And with this tree and others they made a good ship.
The ship, it was launched; but in sight of the land
Such a storm there did rise as no ship could withstand.
It bulged on a rock, and the waves rush'd in fast:
Round and round flew the Raven, and cawed to the blast.
He heard the last shriek of the perishing souls–
See! see! o'er the topmast the mad water rolls!
  Right glad was the Raven, and off he went fleet,
And Death riding home on a cloud he did meet,
And he thank'd him again and again for this treat:
They had taken his all, and Revenge it was sweet!

1797.

A CHRISTMAS CAROL

I

The shepherds went their hasty way,
    And found the lowly stable-shed
Where the Virgin-Mother lay:
    And now they checked their eager tread,
For to the Babe, that at her bosom clung,
A Mother's song the Virgin-Mother sung.

II

They told her how a glorious light,
    Streaming from a heavenly throng,
Around them shone, suspending night!
    While sweeter than a mother's song,
Blest Angels heralded the Saviour's birth,
Glory to God on high! and Peace on Earth.

III

She listened to the tale divine,
  And closer still the Babe she pressed;
And while she cried, the Babe is mine!
  The milk rushed faster to her breast:
Joy rose within her, like a summer's morn;
Peace, Peace on Earth! the Prince of Peace is born.

IV

Thou Mother of the Prince of Peace,
  Poor, simple, and of low estate!
That strife should vanish, battle cease,
  O why should this thy soul elate?
Sweet Music's loudest note, the Poet's story,–
Didst thou ne'er love to hear of fame and glory?

V

And is not War a youthful king,
  A stately Hero clad in mail?
Beneath his footsteps laurels spring;
  Him Earth's majestic monarchs hail
Their friend, their playmate! and his bold bright eye
Compels the maiden's love-confessing sigh.

VI

'Tell this in some more courtly scene,
To maids and youths in robes of state!
I am a woman poor and mean,
And therefore is my soul elate.
War is a ruffian, all with guilt defiled,
That from the agéd father tears his child!

VII

'A murderous fiend, by fiends adored,
He kills the sire and starves the son;
The husband kills, and from her board
Steals all his widow's toil had won;
Plunders God's world of beauty; rends away
All safety from the night, all comfort from the day.

VIII

'Then wisely is my soul elate,
That strife should vanish, battle cease:
I'm poor and of a low estate,
The Mother of the Prince of Peace.
Joy rises in me, like a summer's morn:
Peace, Peace on Earth! the Prince of Peace is born.'

1799.

INSCRIPTION FOR A SEAT BY THE ROAD SIDE HALF-WAY UP A STEEP HILL FACING SOUTH

Thou who in youthful vigour rich, and light
With youthful thoughts dost need no rest! O thou,
To whom alike the valley and the hill
Present a path of ease! Should e'er thine eye
Glance on this sod, and this rude tablet, stop!
'Tis a rude spot, yet here, with thankful hearts,
The foot-worn soldier and his family
Have rested, wife and babe, and boy, perchance
Some eight years old or less, and scantly fed,
Garbed like his father, and already bound
To his poor father's trade. Or think of him
Who, laden with his implements of toil,
Returns at night to some far distant home,
And having plodded on through rain and mire
With limbs o'erlaboured, weak from feverish heat,
And chafed and fretted by December blasts,
Here pauses, thankful he hath reached so far,
And 'mid the sheltering warmth of these bleak trees
Finds restoration–or reflect on those

Who in the spring to meet the warmer sun
Crawl up this steep hill-side, that needlessly
Bends double their weak frames, already bowed
By age or malady, and when, at last,
They gain this wished-for turf, this seat of sods,
Repose–and, well-admonished, ponder here
On final rest. And if a serious thought
Should come uncalled–how soon *thy* motions high,
Thy balmy spirits and thy fervid blood
Must change to feeble, withered, cold and dry,
Cherish the wholesome sadness! And where'er
The tide of Life impel thee, O be prompt
To make thy present strength the staff of all,
Their staff and resting-place–so shalt thou give
To Youth the sweetest joy that Youth can know;
And for thy future self thou shalt provide
Through every change of various life, a seat,
Not built by hands, on which thy inner part,
Imperishable, many a grievous hour,
Or bleak or sultry may repose–yea, sleep
The sleep of Death, and dream of blissful worlds,
Then wake in Heaven, and find the dream all true.

1800.

ODE TO TRANQUILLITY

Tranquillity! thou better name
Than all the family of Fame!
Thou ne'er wilt leave my riper age
To low intrigue, or factious rage;
For oh! dear child of thoughtful Truth,
To thee I gave my early youth,
And left the bark, and blest the steadfast shore,
Ere yet the tempest rose and scared me with its roar.

Who late and lingering seeks thy shrine,
On him but seldom, Power divine,
Thy spirit rests! Satiety
And Sloth, poor counterfeits of thee,
Mock the tired worldling. Idle Hope
And dire Remembrance interlope,
To vex the feverish slumbers of the mind:
The bubble floats before, the spectre stalks behind.

But me thy gentle hand will lead
At morning through the accustomed mead;
And in the sultry summer's heat
Will build me up a mossy seat;

And when the gust of Autumn crowds,
And breaks the busy moonlight clouds,
Thou best the thought canst raise, the heart attune,
Light as the busy clouds, calm as the gliding moon.

The feeling heart, the searching soul,
To thee I dedicate the whole!
And while within myself I trace
The greatness of some future race,
Aloof with hermit-eye I scan
The present works of present man–
A wild and dream-like trade of blood and guile,
Too foolish for a tear, too wicked for a smile!

1801.

AN ODE TO THE RAIN

Composed before daylight, on the morning appointed for the departure of a very worthy, but not very pleasant visitor, whom it was feared the rain might detain.

I

I know it is dark; and though I have lain,
Awake, as I guess, an hour or twain,
I have not once opened the lids of my eyes,
But I lie in the dark, as a blind man lies.
O Rain! that I lie listening to,
  You're but a doleful sound at best:
I owe you little thanks, 'tis true,
  For breaking thus my needful rest!
Yet if, as soon as it is light,
O Rain! you will but take your flight,
I'll neither rail, nor malice keep,
Though sick and sore for want of sleep.
But only now, for this one day,
Do go, dear Rain! do go away!

II

O Rain! with your dull two-fold sound,
The clash hard by, and the murmur all round!
You know, if you know aught, that we,
Both night and day, but ill agree:
For days and months, and almost years,
Have limped on through this vale of tears,
Since body of mine, and rainy weather,
Have lived on easy terms together.
Yet if, as soon as it is light,
O Rain! you will but take your flight,
Though you should come again to-morrow,
And bring with you both pain and sorrow;
Though stomach should sicken and knees should swell–
I'll nothing speak of you but well.
But only now for this one day,
Do go, dear Rain! do go away!

III

Dear Rain! I ne'er refused to say
You're a good creature in your way;
Nay, I could write a book myself,
Would fit a parson's lower shelf,
Showing how very good you are.–
What then? sometimes it must be fair
And if sometimes, why not to-day?
Do go, dear Rain! do go away!

IV

Dear Rain! if I've been cold and shy,
Take no offence! I'll tell you why.
A dear old Friend e'en now is here,
And with him came my sister dear;
After long absence now first met,
Long months by pain and grief beset–
We three dear friends! in truth, we groan
Impatiently to be alone.
We three, you mark! and not one more!
The strong wish makes my spirit sore.
We have so much to talk about,
So many sad things to let out;
So many tears in our eye-corners,
Sitting like little Jacky Horners–
In short, as soon as it is day,
Do go, dear Rain! do go away.

V

And this I'll swear to you, dear Rain!
Whenever you shall come again,
Be you as dull as e'er you could
(And by the bye 'tis understood,
You're not so pleasant as you're good),
Yet, knowing well your worth and place,
I'll welcome you with cheerful face;
And though you stayed a week or more,
Were ten times duller than before;
Yet with kind heart, and right good will,
I'll sit and listen to you still;

Nor should you go away, dear Rain!
Uninvited to remain.
But only now, for this one day,
Do go, dear Rain! do go away.

1802.

THE PAINS OF SLEEP

Ere on my bed my limbs I lay,
It hath not been my use to pray
With moving lips or bended knees;
But silently, by slow degrees,
My spirit I to Love compose,
In humble trust mine eye-lids close,
With reverential resignation,
No wish conceived, no thought exprest,
Only a sense of supplication;
A sense o'er all my soul imprest
That I am weak, yet not unblest,
Since in me, round me, every where
Eternal Strength and Wisdom are.

But yester-night I prayed aloud
In anguish and in agony,
Up-starting from the fiendish crowd
Of shapes and thoughts that tortured me:
A lurid light, a trampling throng,
Sense of intolerable wrong,
And whom I scorned, those only strong!
Thirst of revenge, the powerless will

Still baffled, and yet burning still!
Desire with loathing strangely mixed
On wild or hateful objects fixed.
Fantastic passions! maddening brawl!
And shame and terror over all!
Deeds to be hid which were not hid,
Which all confused I could not know
Whether I suffered, or I did:
For all seemed guilt, remorse or woe,
My own or others still the same
Life-stifling fear, soul-stifling shame.

So two nights passed: the night's dismay
Saddened and stunned the coming day.
Sleep, the wide blessing, seemed to me
Distemper's worst calamity.
The third night, when my own loud scream
Had waked me from the fiendish dream,
O'ercome with sufferings strange and wild,
I wept as I had been a child;
And having thus by tears subdued
My anguish to a milder mood,
Such punishments, I said, were due
To natures deepliest stained with sin,–
For aye entempesting anew
The unfathomable hell within,
The horror of their deeds to view,
To know and loathe, yet wish and do!
Such griefs with such men well agree,
But wherefore, wherefore fall on me?
To be beloved is all I need,
And whom I love, I love indeed.

1803.

FAREWELL TO LOVE

Farewell, sweet Love! yet blame you not my truth;
   More fondly ne'er did mother eye her child
Than I your form: *yours* were my hopes of youth,
   And as *you* shaped my thoughts I sighed or smiled.

While most were wooing wealth, or gaily swerving
   To pleasure's secret haunts, and some apart
Stood strong in pride, self-conscious of deserving,
   To you I gave my whole weak wishing heart.

And when I met the maid that realised
   Your fair creations, and had won her kindness,
Say, but for her if aught on earth I prized!
   Your dreams alone I dreamt, and caught your blindness.

O grief!—but farewell, Love! I will go play me
With thoughts that please me less, and less betray me.

1806.

THE VISIONARY HOPE

Sad lot, to have no Hope! Though lowly kneeling
He fain would frame a prayer within his breast,
Would fain entreat for some sweet breath of healing,
That his sick body might have ease and rest;
He strove in vain! the dull sighs from his chest
Against his will the stifling load revealing,
Though Nature forced; though like some captive guest,
Some royal prisoner at his conqueror's feast,
An alien's restless mood but half concealing,
The sternness on his gentle brow confessed,
Sickness within and miserable feeling:
Though obscure pangs made curses of his dreams,
And dreaded sleep, each night repelled in vain,
Each night was scattered by its own loud screams:
Yet never could his heart command, though fain,
One deep full wish to be no more in pain.

That Hope, which was his inward bliss and boast,
Which waned and died, yet ever near him stood,
Though changed in nature, wander where he would–
For Love's Despair is but Hope's pining Ghost!

For this one hope he makes his hourly moan,
He wishes and can wish for this alone!
Pierced, as with light from Heaven, before its gleams
(So the love-stricken visionary deems)
Disease would vanish, like a summer shower,
Whose dews fling sunshine from the noon-tide bower!
Or let it stay! yet this one Hope should give
Such strength that he would bless his pains and live.

? 1810.

GOD'S OMNIPRESENCE

A HYMN

My Maker! of thy power the trace
In every creature's form and face
    The wond'ring soul surveys:
Thy wisdom, infinite above
Seraphic thought, a Father's love
    As infinite displays!

From all that meets or eye or ear,
There falls a genial holy fear
Which, like the heavy dew of morn,
Refreshes while it bows the heart forlorn!

Great God! thy works how wondrous fair!
Yet sinful man didst thou declare
    The whole Earth's voice and mind!
    If rootless thus, thus substanceless thy state,
Lord, ev'n as Thou all-present art,
O may we still with heedful heart
    Thy presence know and find!

Then, come what will, of weal or woe,
Joy's bosom-spring shall steady flow;
For though 'tis Heaven Thyself to see,
Where but thy *Shadow* falls, Grief cannot be!–

1814.

TO NATURE

It may indeed be phantasy, when I
   Essay to draw from all created things
   Deep, heartfelt, inward joy that closely clings;
And trace in leaves and flowers that round me lie
Lessons of love and earnest piety.
   So let it be; and if the wide world rings
   In mock of this belief, it brings
Nor fear, nor grief, nor vain perplexity.
So will I build my altar in the fields,
   And the blue sky my fretted dome shall be,
And the sweet fragrance that the wild flower yields
   Shall be the incense I will yield to Thee,
Thee only God! and thou shalt not despise
Even me, the priest of this poor sacrifice.

? 1820.

YOUTH AND AGE

Verse, a breeze mid blossoms straying,
Where Hope clung feeding, like a bee–
Both were mine! Life went a-maying
With Nature, Hope, and Poesy,
When I was young!
When I was young?–Ah, woful When!
Ah! for the change 'twixt Now and Then!
This breathing house not built with hands,
This body that does me grievous wrong,
O'er aery cliffs and glittering sands,
How lightly then it flashed along:–
Like those trim skiffs, unknown of yore,
On winding lakes and rivers wide,
That ask no aid of sail or oar,
That fear no spite of wind or tide!
Nought cared this body for wind or weather
When Youth and I lived in't together.

Flowers are lovely; Love is flower-like;
Friendship is a sheltering tree;

O! the joys, that came down shower-like.
Of Friendship, Love, and Liberty,
Ere I was old!
Ere I was old? Ah woful Ere,
Which tells me, Youth's no longer here!
O Youth! for years so many and sweet,
'Tis known, that Thou and I were one,
I'll think it but a fond conceit–
It cannot be that Thou art gone!
Thy vesper-bell hath not yet toll'd:–
And thou wert aye a masker bold!
What strange disguise hast now put on,
To make believe, that thou art gone?
I see these locks in silvery slips,
This drooping gait, this altered size:
But Spring-tide blossoms on thy lips.
And tears take sunshine from thine eyes!
Life is but thought: so think I will
That Youth and I are house-mates still.

Dew-drops are the gems of morning,
But the tears of mournful eve!
Where no hope is, life's a warning
That only serves to make us grieve,
When we are old:
That only serves to make us grieve
With oft and tedious taking-leave,
Like some poor nigh-related guest,
That may not rudely be dismist;
Yet hath outstay'd his welcome while,
And tells the jest without the smile.

1823–1832.

WORK WITHOUT HOPE

LINES COMPOSED
21ST FEBRUARY 1825

All Nature seems at work. Slugs leave their lair–
The bees are stirring–birds are on the wing–
And Winter slumbering in the open air,
Wears on his smiling face a dream of Spring!
And I the while, the sole unbusy thing,
Nor honey make, nor pair, nor build, nor sing.

Yet well I ken the banks where amaranths blow,
Have traced the fount whence streams of nectar flow.
Bloom, O ye amaranths! bloom for whom ye may,
For me ye bloom not! Glide, rich streams, away!
With lips unbrightened, wreathless brow, I stroll:
And would you learn the spells that drowse my soul?
Work without Hope draws nectar in a sieve,
And Hope without an object cannot live.

1825.

DUTY SURVIVING SELF-LOVE

THE ONLY SURE FRIEND OF DECLINING LIFE. A SOLILOQUY

Unchanged within, to see all changed without,
Is a blank lot and hard to bear, no doubt.
Yet why at others' wanings should'st thou fret?
Then only might'st thou feel a just regret,
Hadst thou withheld thy love or hid thy light
In selfish forethought of neglect and slight.
O wiselier then, from feeble yearnings freed,
While, and on whom, thou may'st–shine on! nor heed
Whether the object by reflected light
Return thy radiance or absorb it quite:
And though thou notest from thy safe recess
Old Friends burn dim, like lamps in noisome air,
Love them for what they are; nor love them less,
Because to thee they are not what they were.

1826.

EPITAPH

Stop, Christian passer-by!–Stop, child of God,
And read with gentle breast. Beneath this sod
A poet lies, or that which once seem'd he.
O, lift one thought in prayer for S. T. C.;
That he who many a year with toil of breath
Found death in life, may here find life in death!
Mercy for praise–to be forgiven for fame
He ask'd, and hoped, through Christ. Do thou the same!

9th November, 1833.

Classic Literature: Words and Phrases
adapted from the Collins English Dictionary

Accoucheur NOUN a male midwife or doctor ❑ *I think my sister must have had some general idea that I was a young offender whom an Accoucheur Policemen had taken up (on my birthday) and delivered over to her* (*Great Expectations* by Charles Dickens)

addled ADJ confused and unable to think properly ❑ *But she counted and counted till she got that addled* (*The Adventures of Huckleberry Finn* by Mark Twain)

admiration NOUN amazement or wonder ❑ *lifting up his hands and eyes by way of admiration* (*Gulliver's Travels* by Jonathan Swift)

afeard ADJ afeard means afraid ❑ *shake it–and don't be afeard* (*The Adventures of Huckleberry Finn* by Mark Twain)

affected VERB affected means to assume the appearance of ❑ *Hadst thou affected sweet divinity* (*Doctor Faustus 5.2* by Christopher Marlowe)

aground ADV when a boat runs aground, it touches the ground in a shallow part of the water and gets stuck ❑ *what kep' you?–boat get aground?* (*The Adventures of Huckleberry Finn* by Mark Twain)

ague NOUN a fever in which the patient has alternate hot and cold shivering fits ❑ *his exposure to the wet and cold had brought on fever and ague* (*Oliver Twist* by Charles Dickens)

alchemy ADJ false or worthless ❑ *all wealth alchemy* (*The Sun Rising* by John Donne)

all alike PHRASE the same all the time ❑ *Love, all alike* (*The Sun Rising* by John Donne)

alow and aloft PHRASE alow means in the lower part or bottom, and aloft means on the top, so alow and aloft means on the top and in the bottom or throughout ❑ *Someone's turned the chest out alow and aloft* (*Treasure Island* by Robert Louis Stevenson)

ambuscade NOUN ambuscade is not a proper word. Tom means an ambush, which is when a group of people attack their enemies, after hiding and waiting for them ❑ *and so we would lie in ambuscade, as he called it* (*The Adventures of Huckleberry Finn* by Mark Twain)

amiable ADJ likeable or pleasant ❑ *Such amiable qualities must speak for themselves* (*Pride and Prejudice* by Jane Austen)

amulet NOUN an amulet is a charm thought to drive away evil spirits. ❑ *uttered phrases at once occult and familiar, like the amulet worn on the heart* (*Silas Marner* by George Eliot)

amusement NOUN here amusement means a strange and disturbing puzzle ❑ *this was an amusement the other way* (*Robinson Crusoe* by Daniel Defoe)

ancient NOUN an ancient was the flag displayed on a ship to show which country it belongs to. It is also called the ensign ❑ *her ancient and pendants out* (*Robinson Crusoe* by Daniel Defoe)

antic ADJ here antic means horrible or grotesque ❑ *armed and dressed after a very antic manner* (*Gulliver's Travels* by Jonathan Swift)

antics NOUN antics is an old word meaning clowns, or people who do silly things to make other people laugh ❑ *And point like antics at his triple crown* (*Doctor Faustus 3.2* by Christopher Marlowe)

appanage NOUN an appanage is a living

allowance ❑ *As if loveliness were not the special prerogative of woman–her legitimate appanage and heritage!* (*Jane Eyre* by Charlotte Brontë)

appended VERB appended means attached or added to ❑ *and these words appended* (*Treasure Island* by Robert Louis Stevenson)

approver NOUN an approver is someone who gives evidence against someone he used to work with ❑ *Mr. Noah Claypole: receiving a free pardon from the Crown in consequence of being admitted approver against Fagin* (*Oliver Twist* by Charles Dickens)

areas NOUN the areas is the space, below street level, in front of the basement of a house ❑ *The Dodger had a vicious propensity, too, of pulling the caps from the heads of small boys and tossing them down areas* (*Oliver Twist* by Charles Dickens)

argument NOUN theme or important idea or subject which runs through a piece of writing ❑ *Thrice needful to the argument which now* (*The Prelude* by William Wordsworth)

artificially ADV artfully or cleverly ❑ *and he with a sharp flint sharpened very artificially* (*Gulliver's Travels* by Jonathan Swift)

artist NOUN here artist means a skilled workman ❑ *This man was a most ingenious artist* (*Gulliver's Travels* by Jonathan Swift)

assizes NOUN assizes were regular court sessions which a visiting judge was in charge of ❑ *you shall hang at the next assizes* (*Treasure Island* by Robert Louis Stevenson)

attraction NOUN gravitation, or Newton's theory of gravitation ❑ *he predicted the same fate to attraction* (*Gulliver's Travels* by Jonathan Swift)

aver VERB to aver is to claim something strongly ❑ *for Jem Rodney, the mole catcher, averred that one evening as he was returning homeward* (*Silas Marner* by George Eliot)

baby NOUN here baby means doll, which is a child's toy that looks like a small person ❑ *and skilful dressing her baby* (*Gulliver's Travels* by Jonathan Swift)

bagatelle NOUN bagatelle is a game rather like billiards and pool ❑ *Breakfast had been ordered at a pleasant little tavern, a mile or so away upon the rising ground beyond the green; and there was a bagatelle board in the room, in case we should desire to unbend our minds after the solemnity.* (*Great Expectations* by Charles Dickens)

bah EXCLAM Bah is an exclamation of frustration or anger ❑ *"Bah," said Scrooge.* (*A Christmas Carol* by Charles Dickens)

bairn NOUN a northern word for child ❑ *Who has taught you those fine words, my bairn?* (*Wuthering Heights* by Emily Brontë)

bait VERB to bait means to stop on a journey to take refreshment ❑ *So, when they stopped to bait the horse, and ate and drank and enjoyed themselves, I could touch nothing that they touched, but kept my fast unbroken.* (*David Copperfield* by Charles Dickens)

balustrade NOUN a balustrade is a row of vertical columns that form railings ❑ *but I mean to say you might have got a hearse up that staircase, and taken it broadwise, with the splinter-bar towards the wall, and the door towards the balustrades: and done it easy* (*A Christmas Carol* by Charles Dickens)

bandbox NOUN a large lightweight box for carrying bonnets or hats ❑ *I am glad I bought my bonnet, if it is only for the fun of having another bandbox* (*Pride and Prejudice* by Jane Austen)

barren NOUN a barren here is a stretch or expanse of barren land ❑ *a line of upright stones, continued the* *length of the barren* (*Wuthering Heights* by Emily Brontë)

basin NOUN a basin was a cup without a handle ❑ *who is drinking his tea out of a basin* (*Wuthering Heights* by Emily Brontë)

battalia NOUN the order of battle ❑ *till I saw part of his army in battalia* (*Gulliver's Travels* by Jonathan Swift)

battery NOUN a Battery is a fort or a place where guns are positioned ❑ *You bring the lot to me, at that old Battery over yonder* (*Great Expectations* by Charles Dickens)

battledore and shuttlecock NOUN The game battledore and shuttlecock was an early version of the game now known as badminton. The aim of the early game was simply to keep the shuttlecock from hitting the ground. ❑ *Battledore and shuttlecock's a wery good game vhen you an't the shuttlecock and two lawyers the battledores, in which case it gets too excitin' to be pleasant* (*Pickwick Papers* by Charles Dickens)

beadle NOUN a beadle was a local official who had power over the poor ❑ *But these impertinences were speedily checked by the evidence of the surgeon, and the testimony of the beadle* (*Oliver Twist* by Charles Dickens)

bearings NOUN the bearings of a place are the measurements or directions that are used to find or locate it ❑ *the bearings of the island* (*Treasure Island* by Robert Louis Stevenson)

beaufet NOUN a beaufet was a sideboard ❑ *and sweet-cake from the beaufet* (*Emma* by Jane Austen)

beck NOUN a beck is a small stream ❑ *a beck which follows the bend of the glen* (*Wuthering Heights* by Emily Brontë)

bedight VERB decorated ❑ *and bedight with Christmas holly stuck into the top.* (*A Christmas Carol* by Charles Dickens)

Bedlam NOUN Bedlam was a lunatic asylum in London which had statues carved by Caius Gabriel Cibber at its entrance ❑ *Bedlam, and those carved maniacs at the gates* (*The Prelude* by William Wordsworth)

beeves NOUN oxen or castrated bulls which are animals used for pulling vehicles or carrying things ❑ *to deliver in every morning six beeves* (*Gulliver's Travels* by Jonathan Swift)

begot VERB created or caused ❑ *Begot in thee* (*On His Mistress* by John Donne)

behoof NOUN behoof means benefit ❑ *"Yes, young man," said he, releasing the handle of the article in question, retiring a step or two from my table, and speaking for the behoof of the landlord and waiter at the door* (*Great Expectations* by Charles Dickens)

berth NOUN a berth is a bed on a boat ❑ *this is the berth for me* (*Treasure Island* by Robert Louis Stevenson)

bevers NOUN a bever was a snack, or small portion of food, eaten between main meals ❑ *that buys me thirty meals a day and ten bevers* (*Doctor Faustus 2.1* by Christopher Marlowe)

bilge water NOUN the bilge is the widest part of a ship's bottom, and the bilge water is the dirty water that collects there ❑ *no gush of bilge-water had turned it to fetid puddle* (*Jane Eyre* by Charlotte Brontë)

bills NOUN bills is an old term meaning prescription. A prescription is the piece of paper on which your doctor writes an order for medicine and which you give to a chemist to get the medicine ❑ *Are not thy bills hung up as monuments* (*Doctor Faustus 1.1* by Christopher Marlowe)

black cap NOUN a judge wore a black cap when he was about to sentence a prisoner to death ❑ *The judge assumed the black cap, and the* *prisoner still stood with the same air and gesture.* (*Oliver Twist* by Charles Dickens)

boot-jack NOUN a wooden device to help take boots off ❑ *The speaker appeared to throw a boot-jack, or some such article, at the person he addressed* (*Oliver Twist* by Charles Dickens)

booty NOUN booty means treasure or prizes ❑ *would be inclined to give up their booty in payment of the dead man's debts* (*Treasure Island* by Robert Louis Stevenson)

Bow Street runner PHRASE Bow Street runners were the first British police force, set up by the author Henry Fielding in the eighteenth century ❑ *as would have convinced a judge or a Bow Street runner* (*Treasure Island* by Robert Louis Stevenson)

brawn NOUN brawn is a dish of meat which is set in jelly ❑ *Heaped up upon the floor, to form a kind of throne, were turkeys, geese, game, poultry, brawn, great joints of meat, suckling-pigs* (*A Christmas Carol* by Charles Dickens)

bray VERB when a donkey brays, it makes a loud, harsh sound ❑ *and she doesn't bray like a jackass* (*The Adventures of Huckleberry Finn* by Mark Twain)

break VERB in order to train a horse you first have to break it ❑ *"If a high-mettled creature like this," said he, "can't be broken by fair means, she will never be good for anything"* (*Black Beauty* by Anna Sewell)

bullyragging VERB bullyragging is an old word which means bullying. To bullyrag someone is to threaten or force someone to do something they don't want to do ❑ *and a lot of loafers bullyragging him for sport* (*The Adventures of Huckleberry Finn* by Mark Twain)

but PREP except for (this) ❑ *but this, all pleasures fancies be* (*The Good-Morrow* by John Donne)

by hand PHRASE by hand was a common expression of the time meaning that baby had been fed either using a spoon or a bottle rather than by breast-feeding ❑ *My sister, Mrs. Joe Gargery, was more than twenty years older than I, and had established a great reputation with herself . . . because she had bought me up "by hand"* (*Great Expectations* by Charles Dickens)

bye-spots NOUN bye-spots are lonely places ❑ *and bye-spots of tales rich with indigenous produce* (*The Prelude* by William Wordsworth)

calico NOUN calico is plain white fabric made from cotton ❑ *There was two old dirty calico dresses* (*The Adventures of Huckleberry Finn* by Mark Twain)

camp-fever NOUN camp-fever was another word for the disease typhus ❑ *during a severe camp-fever* (*Emma* by Jane Austen)

cant NOUN cant is insincere or empty talk ❑ *"Man," said the Ghost, "if man you be in heart, not adamant, forbear that wicked cant until you have discovered What the surplus is, and Where it is."* (*A Christmas Carol* by Charles Dickens)

canty ADJ canty means lively, full of life ❑ *My mother lived til eighty, a canty dame to the last* (*Wuthering Heights* by Emily Brontë)

canvas VERB to canvas is to discuss ❑ *We think so very differently on this point Mr Knightley, that there can be no use in canvassing it* (*Emma* by Jane Austen)

capital ADJ capital means excellent or extremely good ❑ *for it's capital, so shady, light, and big* (*Little Women* by Louisa May Alcott)

capstan NOUN a capstan is a device used on a ship to lift sails and anchors ❑ *capstans going, ships going out to sea, and unintelligible sea creatures roaring curses over the bulwarks at respondent lightermen*

(*Great Expectations* by Charles Dickens)

case-bottle NOUN a square bottle designed to fit with others into a case ❑ *The spirit being set before him in a huge case-bottle, which had originally come out of some ship's locker* (*The Old Curiosity Shop* by Charles Dickens)

casement NOUN casement is a word meaning window. The teacher in *Nicholas Nickleby* misspells window showing what a bad teacher he is ❑ *W-i-n, win, d-e-r, der, winder, a casement.* (*Nicholas Nickleby* by Charles Dickens)

cataleptic ADJ a cataleptic fit is one in which the victim goes into a trancelike state and remains still for a long time ❑ *It was at this point in their history that Silas's cataleptic fit occurred during the prayer-meeting* (*Silas Marner* by George Eliot)

cauldron NOUN a cauldron is a large cooking pot made of metal ❑ *stirring a large cauldron which seemed to be full of soup* (*Alice's Adventures in Wonderland* by Lewis Carroll)

cephalic ADJ cephalic means to do with the head ❑ *with ink composed of a cephalic tincture* (*Gulliver's Travels* by Jonathan Swift)

chaise and four NOUN a closed four-wheel carriage pulled by four horses ❑ *he came down on Monday in a chaise and four to see the place* (*Pride and Prejudice* by Jane Austen)

chamberlain NOUN the main servant in a household ❑ *In those times a bed was always to be got there at any hour of the night, and the chamberlain, letting me in at his ready wicket, lighted the candle next in order on his shelf* (*Great Expectations* by Charles Dickens)

characters NOUN distinguishing marks ❑ *Impressed upon all forms the characters* (*The Prelude* by William Wordsworth)

chary ADJ cautious ❑ *I should have been chary of discussing my guardian too freely even with her* (*Great Expectations* by Charles Dickens)

cherishes VERB here cherishes means cheers or brightens ❑ *some philosophic song of Truth that cherishes our daily life* (*The Prelude* by William Wordsworth)

chickens' meat PHRASE chickens' meat is an old term which means chickens' feed or food ❑ *I had shook a bag of chickens' meat out in that place* (*Robinson Crusoe* by Daniel Defoe)

chimeras NOUN a chimera is an unrealistic idea or a wish which is unlikely to be fulfilled ❑ *with many other wild impossible chimeras* (*Gulliver's Travels* by Jonathan Swift)

chines NOUN chine is a cut of meat that includes part or all of the backbone of the animal ❑ *and they found hams and chines uncut* (*Silas Marner* by George Eliot)

chits NOUN chits is a slang word which means girls ❑ *I hate affected, niminy-piminy chits!* (*Little Women* by Louisa May Alcott)

chopped VERB chopped means come suddenly or accidentally ❑ *if I had chopped upon them* (*Robinson Crusoe* by Daniel Defoe)

chute NOUN a narrow channel ❑ *One morning about day-break, I found a canoe and crossed over a chute to the main shore* (*The Adventures of Huckleberry Finn* by Mark Twain)

circumspection NOUN careful observation of events and circumstances; caution ❑ *I honour your circumspection* (*Pride and Prejudice* by Jane Austen)

clambered VERB clambered means to climb somewhere with difficulty, usually using your hands and your feet ❑ *he clambered up and down stairs* (*Treasure Island* by Robert Louis Stevenson)

clime NOUN climate ❑ *no season knows nor clime* (*The Sun Rising* by John Donne)

clinched VERB clenched ❑ *the tops whereof I could but just reach with my fist clinched* (*Gulliver's Travels* by Jonathan Swift)

close chair NOUN a close chair is a sedan chair, which is an covered chair which has room for one person. The sedan chair is carried on two poles by two men, one in front and one behind ❑ *persuaded even the Empress herself to let me hold her in her close chair* (*Gulliver's Travels* by Jonathan Swift)

clown NOUN clown here means peasant or person who lives off the land ❑ *In ancient days by emperor and clown* (*Ode on a Nightingale* by John Keats)

coalheaver NOUN a coalheaver loaded coal onto ships using a spade ❑ *Good, strong, wholesome medicine, as was given with great success to two Irish labourers and a coalheaver* (*Oliver Twist* by Charles Dickens)

coal-whippers NOUN men who worked at docks using machines to load coal onto ships ❑ *here, were colliers by the score and score, with the coal-whippers plunging off stages on deck* (*Great Expectations* by Charles Dickens)

cobweb NOUN a cobweb is the net which a spider makes for catching insects ❑ *the walls and ceilings were all hung round with cobwebs* (*Gulliver's Travels* by Jonathan Swift)

coddling VERB coddling means to treat someone too kindly or protect them too much ❑ *and I've been coddling the fellow as if I'd been his grand-mother* (*Little Women* by Louisa May Alcott)

coil NOUN coil means noise or fuss or disturbance ❑ *What a coil is there?* (*Doctor Faustus 4.7* by Christopher Marlowe)

collared VERB to collar something is a slang term which means to capture. In this sentence, it means he stole it [the money] ❑ *he collared it* (*The Adventures of Huckleberry Finn* by Mark Twain)

colling VERB colling is an old word which means to embrace and kiss ❑ *and no clasping and colling at all* (*Tess of the D'Urbervilles* by Thomas Hardy)

colloquies NOUN colloquy is a formal conversation or dialogue ❑ *Such colloquies have occupied many a pair of pale-faced weavers* (*Silas Marner* by George Eliot)

comfit NOUN sugar-covered pieces of fruit or nut eaten as sweets ❑ *and pulled out a box of comfits* (*Alice's Adventures in Wonderland* by Lewis Carroll)

coming out VERB when a girl came out in society it meant she was of marriageable age. In order to "come out" girls were expecting to attend balls and other parties during a season ❑ *The younger girls formed hopes of coming out a year or two sooner than they might otherwise have done* (*Pride and Prejudice* by Jane Austen)

commit VERB commit means arrest or stop ❑ *Commit the rascals* (*Doctor Faustus 4.7* by Christopher Marlowe)

commodious ADJ commodious means convenient ❑ *the most commodious and effectual ways* (*Gulliver's Travels* by Jonathan Swift)

commons NOUN commons is an old term meaning food shared with others ❑ *his pauper assistants ranged themselves behind him; the gruel was served out; and a long grace was said over the short commons.* (*Oliver Twist* by Charles Dickens)

complacency NOUN here complacency means a desire to please others. To-day complacency means feeling pleased with oneself without good reason. ❑ *Twas thy power that raised the first complacency in me* (*The Prelude* by William Wordsworth)

complaisance NOUN complaisance was eagerness to please ❑ *we cannot wonder at his complaisance* (*Pride and Prejudice* by Jane Austen)

complaisant ADJ complaisant means polite ❑ *extremely cheerful and complaisant to their guest* (*Gulliver's Travels* by Jonathan Swift)

conning VERB conning means learning by heart ❑ *Or conning more* (*The Prelude* by William Wordsworth)

consequent NOUN consequence ❑ *as avarice is the necessary consequent of old age* (*Gulliver's Travels* by Jonathan Swift)

consorts NOUN concerts ❑ *The King, who delighted in music, had frequent consorts at Court* (*Gulliver's Travels* by Jonathan Swift)

conversible ADJ conversible meant easy to talk to, companionable ❑ *He can be a conversible companion* (*Pride and Prejudice* by Jane Austen)

copper NOUN a copper is a large pot that can be heated directly over a fire ❑ *He gazed in stupefied astonishment on the small rebel for some seconds, and then clung for support to the copper* (*Oliver Twist* by Charles Dickens)

copper-stick NOUN a copper-stick is the long piece of wood used to stir washing in the copper (or boiler) which was usually the biggest cooking pot in the house ❑ *It was Christmas Eve, and I had to stir the pudding for next day, with a copper-stick, from seven to eight by the Dutch clock* (*Great Expectations* by Charles Dickens)

counting-house NOUN a counting-house is a place where accountants work ❑ *Once upon a time–of all the good days in the year, on Christmas Eve–old Scrooge sat busy in his counting-house* (*A Christmas Carol* by Charles Dickens)

courtier NOUN a courtier is someone who attends the king or queen–a member of the court ❑ *next the ten courtiers;* (*Alice's Adventures in Wonderland* by Lewis Carroll)

covies NOUN covies were flocks of partridges ❑ *and will save all of the best covies for you* (*Pride and Prejudice* by Jane Austen)

cowed VERB cowed means frightened or intimidated ❑ *it cowed me more than the pain* (*Treasure Island* by Robert Louis Stevenson)

cozened VERB cozened means tricked or deceived ❑ *Do you remember, sir, how you cozened me* (*Doctor Faustus 4.7* by Christopher Marlowe)

cravats NOUN a cravat is a folded cloth that a man wears wrapped around his neck as a decorative item of clothing ❑ *we'd 'a' slept in our cravats to-night* (*The Adventures of Huckleberry Finn* by Mark Twain)

crock and dirt PHRASE crock and dirt is an old expression meaning soot and dirt ❑ *and the mare catching cold at the door, and the boy grimed with crock and dirt* (*Great Expectations* by Charles Dickens)

crockery NOUN here crockery means pottery ❑ *By one of the parrots was a cat made of crockery* (*The Adventures of Huckleberry Finn* by Mark Twain)

crooked sixpence PHRASE it was considered unlucky to have a bent sixpence ❑ *You've got the beauty, you see, and I've got the luck, so you must keep me by you for your crooked sixpence* (*Silas Marner* by George Eliot)

croquet NOUN croquet is a traditional English summer game in which players try to hit wooden balls through hoops ❑ *and once she remembered trying to box her own ears for having cheated herself in a game of croquet* (*Alice's Adventures in Wonderland* by Lewis Carroll)

cross PREP across ❑ The two great streets, which run cross and divide it into four quarters (*Gulliver's Travels* by Jonathan Swift)

culpable ADJ if you are culpable for something it means you are to blame ❑ *deep are the sorrows that spring from false ideas for which no man is culpable.* (*Silas Marner* by George Eliot)

cultured ADJ cultivated ❑ *Nor less when spring had warmed the cultured Vale* (*The Prelude* by William Wordsworth)

cupidity NOUN cupidity is greed ❑ *These people hated me with the hatred of cupidity and disappointment.* (*Great Expectations* by Charles Dickens)

curricle NOUN an open two-wheeled carriage with one seat for the driver and space for a single passenger ❑ *and they saw a lady and a gentleman in a curricle* (*Pride and Prejudice* by Jane Austen)

cynosure NOUN a cynosure is something that strongly attracts attention or admiration ❑ *Then I thought of Eliza and Georgiana; I beheld one the cynosure of a ballroom, the other the inmate of a convent cell* (*Jane Eyre* by Charlotte Brontë)

dalliance NOUN someone's dalliance with something is a brief involvement with it ❑ *nor sporting in the dalliance of love* (*Doctor Faustus Chorus* by Christopher Marlowe)

darkling ADV darkling is an archaic way of saying in the dark ❑ *Darkling I listen* (*Ode on a Nightingale* by John Keats)

delf-case NOUN a sideboard for holding dishes and crockery ❑ *at the pewter dishes and delf-case* (*Wuthering Heights* by Emily Brontë)

determined ■ VERB here determined means ended ❑ *and be out of vogue when that was determined* (*Gulliver's Travels* by Jonathan Swift) ■ VERB determined can mean to have been learned or found especially by investigation or experience ❑ *All the sensitive feelings it wounded so cruelly, all the shame and misery it kept alive within my breast, became more poignant as I thought of this; and I determined that the life was unendurable* (*David Copperfield* by Charles Dickens)

Deuce NOUN a slang term for the Devil ❑ *Ah, I dare say I did. Deuce take me, he added suddenly, I know I did. I find I am not quite unscrewed yet.* (*Great Expectations* by Charles Dickens)

diabolical ADJ diabolical means devilish or evil ❑ *and with a thousand diabolical expressions* (*Treasure Island* by Robert Louis Stevenson)

direction NOUN here direction means address ❑ *Elizabeth was not surprised at it, as Jane had written the direction remarkably ill* (*Pride and Prejudice* by Jane Austen)

discover VERB to make known or announce ❑ *the Emperor would discover the secret while I was out of his power* (*Gulliver's Travels* by Jonathan Swift)

dissemble VERB hide or conceal ❑ *Dissemble nothing* (*On His Mistress* by John Donne)

dissolve VERB dissolve here means to release from life, to die ❑ *Fade far away, dissolve, and quite forget* (*Ode on a Nightingale* by John Keats)

distrain VERB to distrain is to seize the property of someone who is in debt in compensation for the money owed ❑ *for he's threatening to distrain for it* (*Silas Marner* by George Eliot)

Divan NOUN a Divan was originally a Turkish council of state–the name was transferred to the couches they sat on and is used to mean this in English ❑ *Mr Brass applauded this picture very much, and the bed being soft and comfortable, Mr Quilp determined to use it, both as a sleeping place by night and as a kind of Divan by day.* (*The Old Curiosity Shop* by Charles Dickens)

divorcement NOUN separation ❑ *By all pains which want and divorcement* *hath* (*On His Mistress* by John Donne)

dog in the manger, PHRASE this phrase describes someone who prevents you from enjoying something that they themselves have no need for ❑ *You are a dog in the manger, Cathy, and desire no one to be loved but yourself* (*Wuthering Heights* by Emily Brontë)

dolorifuge NOUN dolorifuge is a word which Thomas Hardy invented. It means pain-killer or comfort ❑ *as a species of dolorifuge* (*Tess of the D'Urbervilles* by Thomas Hardy)

dome NOUN building ❑ *that river and that mouldering dome* (*The Prelude* by William Wordsworth)

domestic NOUN here domestic means a person's management of the house ❑ *to give some account of my domestic* (*Gulliver's Travels* by Jonathan Swift)

dunce NOUN a dunce is another word for idiot ❑ *Do you take me for a dunce? Go on?* (*Alice's Adventures in Wonderland* by Lewis Carroll)

Ecod EXCLAM a slang exclamation meaning "oh God!" ❑ *"Ecod," replied Wemmick, shaking his head, "that's not my trade."* (*Great Expectations* by Charles Dickens)

egg-hot NOUN an egg-hot (see also "flip" and "negus") was a hot drink made from beer and eggs, sweetened with nutmeg ❑ *She fainted when she saw me return, and made a little jug of egg-hot afterwards to console us while we talked it over.* (*David Copperfield* by Charles Dickens)

encores NOUN an encore is a short extra performance at the end of a longer one, which the entertainer gives because the audience has enthusiastically asked for it ❑ *we want a little something to answer encores with, anyway* (*The Adventures of Huckleberry Finn* by Mark Twain)

equipage NOUN an elegant and impressive carriage ❑ *and besides, the equipage did not answer to any of their neighbours* (*Pride and Prejudice* by Jane Austen)

exordium NOUN an exordium is the opening part of a speech ❑ *"Now, Handel," as if it were the grave beginning of a portentous business exordium, he had suddenly given up that tone* (*Great Expectations* by Charles Dickens)

expect VERB here expect means to wait for ❑ *to expect his farther commands* (*Gulliver's Travels* by Jonathan Swift)

familiars NOUN familiars means spirits or devils who come to someone when they are called ❑ *I'll turn all the lice about thee into familiars* (*Doctor Faustus 1.4* by Christopher Marlowe)

fantods NOUN a fantod is a person who fidgets or can't stop moving nervously ❑ *It most give me the fantods* (*The Adventures of Huckleberry Finn* by Mark Twain)

farthing NOUN a farthing is an old unit of British currency which was worth a quarter of a penny ❑ *Not a farthing less. A great many back-payments are included in it, I assure you.* (*A Christmas Carol* by Charles Dickens)

farthingale NOUN a hoop worn under a skirt to extend it ❑ *A bell with an old voice–which I dare say in its time had often said to the house, Here is the green farthingale* (*Great Expectations* by Charles Dickens)

favours NOUN here favours is an old word which means ribbons ❑ *A group of humble mourners entered the gate: wearing white favours* (*Oliver Twist* by Charles Dickens)

feigned VERB pretend or pretending ❑ *not my feigned page* (*On His Mistress* by John Donne)

fence ■ NOUN a fence is someone who receives and sells stolen goods ❑ *What are you up to? Ill-treating the boys, you covetous, avaricious, in-sa-ti-a-ble old fence?* (*Oliver Twist* by

Charles Dickens) ■ NOUN defence or protection ❑ *but honesty hath no fence against superior cunning* (*Gulliver's Travels* by Jonathan Swift)

fess ADJ fess is an old word which means pleased or proud ❑ *You'll be fess enough, my poppet* (*Tess of the D'Urbervilles* by Thomas Hardy)

fettered ADJ fettered means bound in chains or chained ❑ *"You are fettered," said Scrooge, trembling. "Tell me why?"* (*A Christmas Carol* by Charles Dickens)

fidges VERB fidges means fidgets, which is to keep moving your hands slightly because you are nervous or excited ❑ *Look, Jim, how my fingers fidges* (*Treasure Island* by Robert Louis Stevenson)

finger-post NOUN a finger-post is a sign-post showing the direction to different places ❑ *"The gallows," continued Fagin, "the gallows, my dear, is an ugly finger-post, which points out a very short and sharp turning that has stopped many a bold fellow's career on the broad highway."* (*Oliver Twist* by Charles Dickens)

fire-irons NOUN fire-irons are tools kept by the side of the fire to either cook with or look after the fire ❑ *the fire-irons came first* (*Alice's Adventures in Wonderland* by Lewis Carroll)

fire-plug NOUN a fire-plug is another word for a fire hydrant ❑ *The pony looked with great attention into a fire-plug, which was near him, and appeared to be quite absorbed in contemplating it* (*The Old Curiosity Shop* by Charles Dickens)

flank NOUN flank is the side of an animal ❑ *And all her silken flanks with garlands dressed* (*Ode on a Grecian Urn* by John Keats)

flip NOUN a flip is a drink made from warmed ale, sugar, spice and beaten egg ❑ *The events of the day, in combination with the twins, if not with the flip, had made Mrs. Micawber hysterical, and she shed tears as she replied* (*David Copperfield* by Charles Dickens)

flit VERB flit means to move quickly ❑ *and if he had meant to flit to Thrushcross Grange* (*Wuthering Heights* by Emily Brontë)

floorcloth NOUN a floorcloth was a hard-wearing piece of canvas used instead of carpet ❑ *This avenging phantom was ordered to be on duty at eight on Tuesday morning in the hall (it was two feet square, as charged for floorcloth)* (*Great Expectations* by Charles Dickens)

fly-driver NOUN a fly-driver is a carriage drawn by a single horse ❑ *The fly-drivers, among whom I inquired next, were equally jocose and equally disrespectful* (*David Copperfield* by Charles Dickens)

fob NOUN a small pocket in which a watch is kept ❑ *"Certain," replied the man, drawing a gold watch from his fob* (*Oliver Twist* by Charles Dickens)

folly NOUN folly means foolishness or stupidity ❑ *the folly of beginning a work* (*Robinson Crusoe* by Daniel Defoe)

fond ADJ fond means foolish ❑ *Fond worldling* (*Doctor Faustus 5.2* by Christopher Marlowe)

fondness NOUN silly or foolish affection ❑ *They have no fondness for their colts or foals* (*Gulliver's Travels* by Jonathan Swift)

for his fancy PHRASE for his fancy means for his liking or as he wanted ❑ *and as I did not obey quick enough for his fancy* (*Treasure Island* by Robert Louis Stevenson)

forlorn ADJ lost or very upset ❑ *you are from that day forlorn* (*Gulliver's Travels* by Jonathan Swift)

foster-sister NOUN a foster-sister was someone brought up by the same nurse or in the same household ❑ *I had been his foster-sister* (*Wuthering Heights* by Emily Brontë)

fox-fire NOUN fox-fire is a weak glow that is given off by decaying, rotten wood ❑ *what we must have was a lot of them rotten chunks that's called fox-fire* (*The Adventures of Huckleberry Finn* by Mark Twain)

frozen sea PHRASE the Arctic Ocean ❑ *into the frozen sea* (*Gulliver's Travels* by Jonathan Swift)

gainsay VERB to gainsay something is to say it isn't true or to deny it ❑ *"So she had," cried Scrooge. "You're right. I'll not gainsay it, Spirit. God forbid!"* (*A Christmas Carol* by Charles Dickens)

gaiters NOUN gaiters were leggings made of a cloth or piece of leather which covered the leg from the knee to the ankle ❑ *Mr Knightley was hard at work upon the lower buttons of his thick leather gaiters* (*Emma* by Jane Austen)

galluses NOUN galluses is an old spelling of gallows, and here means suspenders. Suspenders are straps worn over someone's shoulders and fastened to their trousers to prevent the trousers falling down ❑ *and home-knit galluses* (*The Adventures of Huckleberry Finn* by Mark Twain)

galoot NOUN a sailor but also a clumsy person ❑ *and maybe a galoot on it chopping* (*The Adventures of Huckleberry Finn* by Mark Twain)

gayest ADJ gayest means the most lively and bright or merry ❑ *Beth played her gayest march* (*Little Women* by Louisa May Alcott)

gem NOUN here gem means jewellery ❑ *the mountain shook off turf and flower, had only heath for raiment and crag for gem* (*Jane Eyre* by Charlotte Brontë)

giddy ADJ giddy means dizzy ❑ *and I wish you wouldn't keep appearing and vanishing so suddenly; you make one quite giddy.* (*Alice's Adventures in Wonderland* by Lewis Carroll)

gig NOUN a light two-wheeled carriage ❑ *when a gig drove up to the garden gate: out of which there jumped a fat gentleman* (*Oliver Twist* by Charles Dickens)

gladsome ADJ gladsome is an old word meaning glad or happy ❑ *Nobody ever stopped him in the street to say, with gladsome looks* (*A Christmas Carol* by Charles Dickens)

glen NOUN a glen is a small valley; the word is used commonly in Scotland ❑ *a beck which follows the bend of the glen* (*Wuthering Heights* by Emily Brontë)

gravelled VERB gravelled is an old term which means to baffle or defeat someone ❑ *Gravelled the pastors of the German Church* (*Doctor Faustus 1.1* by Christopher Marlowe)

grinder NOUN a grinder was a private tutor ❑ *but that when he had had the happiness of marrying Mrs Pocket very early in his life, he had impaired his prospects and taken up the calling of a Grinder* (*Great Expectations* by Charles Dickens)

gruel NOUN gruel is a thin, watery cornmeal or oatmeal soup ❑ *and the little saucepan of gruel (Scrooge had a cold in his head) upon the hob.* (*A Christmas Carol* by Charles Dickens)

guinea, half a NOUN half a guinea was ten shillings and sixpence ❑ *but lay out half a guinea at Ford's* (*Emma* by Jane Austen)

gull VERB gull is an old term which means to fool or deceive someone ❑ *Hush, I'll gull him supernaturally* (*Doctor Faustus 3.4* by Christopher Marlowe)

gunnel NOUN the gunnel, or gunwale, is the upper edge of a boat's side ❑ *But he put his foot on the gunnel and rocked her* (*The Adventures of Huckleberry Finn* by Mark Twain)

gunwale NOUN the side of a ship ❑ *He dipped his hand in the water over the boat's gunwale* (*Great Expectations* by Charles Dickens)

Gytrash NOUN a Gytrash is an omen of misfortune to the superstitious, usually taking the form of a hound ❑ *I remembered certain of Bessie's tales, wherein figured a North-of-England spirit, called a "Gytrash"* (*Jane Eyre* by Charlotte Brontë)

hackney-cabriolet NOUN a two-wheeled carriage with four seats for hire and pulled by a horse ❑ *A hackney-cabriolet was in waiting; with the same vehemence which she had exhibited in addressing Oliver, the girl pulled him in with her, and drew the curtains close.* (*Oliver Twist* by Charles Dickens)

hackney-coach NOUN a four-wheeled horse-drawn vehicle for hire ❑ *The twilight was beginning to close in, when Mr. Brownlow alighted from a hackney-coach at his own door, and knocked softly.* (*Oliver Twist* by Charles Dickens)

haggler NOUN a haggler is someone who travels from place to place selling small goods and items ❑ *when I be plain Jack Durbeyfield, the haggler* (*Tess of the D'Urbervilles* by Thomas Hardy)

halter NOUN a halter is a rope or strap used to lead an animal or to tie it up ❑ *I had of course long been used to a halter and a headstall* (*Black Beauty* by Anna Sewell)

hamlet NOUN a hamlet is a small village or a group of houses in the countryside ❑ *down from the hamlet* (*Treasure Island* by Robert Louis Stevenson)

hand-barrow NOUN a hand-barrow is a device for carrying heavy objects. It is like a wheelbarrow except that it has handles, rather than wheels, for moving the barrow ❑ *his sea chest following behind him in a hand-barrow* (*Treasure Island* by Robert Louis Stevenson)

handspike NOUN a handspike was a stick which was used as a lever ❑ *a bit of stick like a handspike* (*Treasure Island* by Robert Louis Stevenson)

haply ADV haply means by chance or perhaps ❑ *And haply the Queen-Moon is on her throne* (*Ode on a Nightingale* by John Keats)

harem NOUN the harem was the part of the house where the women lived ❑ *mostly they hang round the harem* (*The Adventures of Huckleberry Finn* by Mark Twain)

hautboys NOUN hautboys are oboes ❑ *sausages and puddings resembling flutes and hautboys* (*Gulliver's Travels* by Jonathan Swift)

hawker NOUN a hawker is someone who sells goods to people as he travels rather than from a fixed place like a shop ❑ *to buy some stockings from a hawker* (*Treasure Island* by Robert Louis Stevenson)

hawser NOUN a hawser is a rope used to tie up or tow a ship or boat ❑ *Again among the tiers of shipping, in and out, avoiding rusty chain-cables, frayed hempen hawsers* (*Great Expectations* by Charles Dickens)

headstall NOUN the headstall is the part of the bridle or halter that goes around a horse's head ❑ *I had of course long been used to a halter and a headstall* (*Black Beauty* by Anna Sewell)

hearken VERB hearken means to listen ❑ *though we sometimes stopped to lay hold of each other and hearken* (*Treasure Island* by Robert Louis Stevenson)

heartless ADJ here heartless means without heart or dejected ❑ *I am not heartless* (*The Prelude* by William Wordsworth)

hebdomadal ADJ hebdomadal means weekly ❑ *It was the hebdomadal treat to which we all looked forward from Sabbath to Sabbath* (*Jane Eyre* by Charlotte Brontë)

highwaymen NOUN highwaymen were people who stopped travellers and robbed them ❑ *We are highwaymen* (*The Adventures of Huckleberry Finn* by Mark Twain)

hinds NOUN hinds means farm hands, or people who work on a farm ❑ *He called his hinds about him* (*Gulliver's Travels* by Jonathan Swift)

histrionic ADJ if you refer to someone's behaviour as histrionic, you are being critical of it because it is dramatic and exaggerated ❑ *But the histrionic muse is the darling* (*The Adventures of Huckleberry Finn* by Mark Twain)

hogs NOUN hogs is another word for pigs ❑ *Tom called the hogs "ingots"* (*The Adventures of Huckleberry Finn* by Mark Twain)

horrors NOUN the horrors are a fit, called delirium tremens, which is caused by drinking too much alcohol ❑ *I'll have the horrors* (*Treasure Island* by Robert Louis Stevenson)

huffy ADJ huffy means to be obviously annoyed or offended about something ❑ *They will feel that more than angry speeches or huffy actions* (*Little Women* by Louisa May Alcott)

hulks NOUN hulks were prison-ships ❑ *The miserable companion of thieves and ruffians, the fallen outcast of low haunts, the associate of the scourings of the jails and hulks* (*Oliver Twist* by Charles Dickens)

humbug NOUN humbug means nonsense or rubbish ❑ *"Bah," said Scrooge. "Humbug!"* (*A Christmas Carol* by Charles Dickens)

humours NOUN it was believed that there were four fluids in the body called humours which decided the temperament of a person depending on how much of each fluid was present ❑ *other peccant humours* (*Gulliver's Travels* by Jonathan Swift)

husbandry NOUN husbandry is farming animals ❑ *bad husbandry were plentifully anointing their wheels* (*Silas Marner* by George Eliot)

huswife NOUN a huswife was a small sewing kit ❑ *but I had put my huswife on it* (*Emma* by Jane Austen)

ideal ADJ ideal in this context means imaginary ❑ *I discovered the yell was not ideal* (*Wuthering Heights* by Emily Brontë)

If our two PHRASE if both our ❑ *If our two loves be one* (*The Good-Morrow* by John Donne)

ignis-fatuus NOUN ignis-fatuus is the light given out by burning marsh gases, which lead careless travellers into danger ❑ *it is madness in all women to let a secret love kindle within them, which, if unreturned and unknown, must devour the life that feeds it; and, if discovered and responded to, must lead ignis-fatuus-like, into miry wilds whence there is no extrication.* (*Jane Eyre* by Charlotte Brontë)

imaginations NOUN here imaginations means schemes or plans ❑ *soon drove out those imaginations* (*Gulliver's Travels* by Jonathan Swift)

impressible ADJ impressible means open or impressionable ❑ *for Marner had one of those impressible, self-doubting natures* (*Silas Marner* by George Eliot)

in good intelligence PHRASE friendly with each other ❑ *that these two persons were in good intelligence with each other* (*Gulliver's Travels* by Jonathan Swift)

inanity NOUN inanity is silliness or dull stupidity ❑ *Do we not wile away moments of inanity* (*Silas Marner* by George Eliot)

incivility NOUN incivility means rudeness or impoliteness ❑ *if it's only for a piece of incivility like to-night's* (*Treasure Island* by Robert Louis Stevenson)

indigenae NOUN indigenae means natives or people from that area ❑ *an exotic that the surly indigenae will not recognise for kin* (*Wuthering Heights* by Emily Brontë)

indocible ADJ unteachable ❑ *so they were the most restive and indocible* (*Gulliver's Travels* by Jonathan Swift)

ingenuity NOUN inventiveness ❑ *entreated me to give him something as an encouragement to ingenuity* (*Gulliver's Travels* by Jonathan Swift)

ingots NOUN an ingot is a lump of a valuable metal like gold, usually shaped like a brick ❑ *Tom called the hogs "ingots"* (*The Adventures of Huckleberry Finn* by Mark Twain)

inkstand NOUN an inkstand is a pot which was put on a desk to contain either ink or pencils and pens ❑ *throwing an inkstand at the Lizard as she spoke* (*Alice's Adventures in Wonderland* by Lewis Carroll)

inordinate ADJ without order. To-day inordinate means "excessive". ❑ *Though yet untutored and inordinate* (*The Prelude* by William Wordsworth)

intellectuals NOUN here intellectuals means the minds (of the workmen) ❑ *those instructions they give being too refined for the intellectuals of their workmen* (*Gulliver's Travels* by Jonathan Swift)

interview NOUN meeting ❑ *By our first strange and fatal interview* (*On His Mistress* by John Donne)

jacks NOUN jacks are rods for turning a spit over a fire ❑ *It was a small bit of pork suspended from the kettle hanger by a string passed through a large door key, in a way known to primitive housekeepers unpossessed of jacks* (*Silas Marner* by George Eliot)

jews-harp NOUN a jews-harp is a small, metal, musical instrument that is played by the mouth ❑ *A jews-harp's plenty good enough for a rat* (*The Adventures of Huckleberry Finn* by Mark Twain)

jorum NOUN a large bowl ❑ *while Miss Skiffins brewed such a jorum of tea, that the pig in the back premises became strongly excited* (*Great Expectations* by Charles Dickens)

jostled VERB jostled means bumped or pushed by someone or some people ❑ *being jostled himself into the kennel* (*Gulliver's Travels* by Jonathan Swift)

keepsake NOUN a keepsake is a gift which reminds someone of an event or of the person who gave it to them. ❑ *books and ornaments they had in their boudoirs at home: keepsakes that different relations had presented to them* (*Jane Eyre* by Charlotte Brontë)

kenned VERB kenned means knew ❑ *though little kenned the lamplighter that he had any company but Christmas!* (*A Christmas Carol* by Charles Dickens)

kennel NOUN kennel means gutter, which is the edge of a road next to the pavement, where rain water collects and flows away ❑ *being jostled himself into the kennel* (*Gulliver's Travels* by Jonathan Swift)

knock-knee ADJ knock-knee means slanted, at an angle. ❑ *LOT 1 was marked in whitewashed knock-knee letters on the brewhouse* (*Great Expectations* by Charles Dickens)

ladylike ADJ to be ladylike is to behave in a polite, dignified and graceful way ❑ *No, winking isn't ladylike* (*Little Women* by Louisa May Alcott)

lapse NOUN flow ❑ *Stealing with silent lapse to join the brook* (*The Prelude* by William Wordsworth)

larry NOUN larry is an old word which means commotion or noisy celebration ❑ *That was all a part of the larry!* (*Tess of the D'Urbervilles* by Thomas Hardy)

laths NOUN laths are strips of wood ❑ *The panels shrunk, the windows cracked; fragments of plaster fell out of the ceiling, and the naked laths were shown instead* (*A Christmas Carol* by Charles Dickens)

leer NOUN a leer is an unpleasant smile ❑ *with a kind of leer* (*Treasure Island* by Robert Louis Stevenson)

lenitives NOUN these are different kinds of drugs or medicines: lenitives and palliatives were pain relievers; aperitives were laxatives; abstersives caused vomiting; corrosives destroyed human tissue; restringents caused constipation; cephalalgics stopped headaches; icterics were used as medicine for jaundice; apophlegmatics were cough medicine, and acoustics were cures for the loss of hearing ❑ *lenitives, aperitives, abstersives, corrosives, restringents, palliatives, laxatives, cephalalgics, icterics, apophlegmatics, acoustics* (*Gulliver's Travels* by Jonathan Swift)

lest CONJ in case. If you do something lest something (usually) unpleasant happens you do it to try to prevent it happening ❑ *She went in without knocking, and hurried upstairs, in great fear lest she should meet the real Mary Ann* (*Alice's Adventures in Wonderland* by Lewis Carroll)

levee NOUN a levee is an old term for a meeting held in the morning, shortly after the person holding the meeting has got out of bed ❑ *I used to attend the King's levee once or twice a week* (*Gulliver's Travels* by Jonathan Swift)

life-preserver NOUN a club which had lead inside it to make it heavier and therefore more dangerous ❑ *and with no more suspicious articles displayed to view than two or three heavy bludgeons which stood in a corner, and a "life-preserver" that hung over the chimney-piece.* (*Oliver Twist* by Charles Dickens)

lighterman NOUN a lighterman is another word for sailor ❑ *in and out, hammers going in ship-builders' yards, saws going at timber, clashing engines going at things unknown, pumps going in leaky ships, capstans going, ships going out to sea, and unintelligible sea creatures roaring curses over the bulwarks at respondent lightermen* (*Great Expectations* by Charles Dickens)

livery NOUN servants often wore a uniform known as a livery ❑ *suddenly a footman in livery came running out of the wood* (*Alice's Adventures in Wonderland* by Lewis Carroll)

livid ADJ livid means pale or ash coloured. Livid also means very angry ❑ *a dirty, livid white* (*Treasure Island* by Robert Louis Stevenson)

lottery-tickets NOUN a popular card game ❑ *and Mrs. Philips protested that they would have a nice comfortable noisy game of lottery tickets* (*Pride and Prejudice* by Jane Austen)

lower and upper world PHRASE the earth and the heavens are the lower and upper worlds ❑ *the changes in the lower and upper world* (*Gulliver's Travels* by Jonathan Swift)

lustres NOUN lustres are chandeliers. A chandelier is a large, decorative frame which holds light bulbs or candles and hangs from the ceiling ❑ *the lustres, lights, the carving and the guilding* (*The Prelude* by William Wordsworth)

lynched VERB killed without a criminal trial by a crowd of people ❑ *He'll never know how nigh he come to getting lynched* (*The Adventures of Huckleberry Finn* by Mark Twain)

malingering VERB if someone is malingering they are pretending to be ill to avoid working ❑ *And you stand there malingering* (*Treasure Island* by Robert Louis Stevenson)

managing PHRASE treating with consideration ❑ *to think the honour of my own kind not worth managing* (*Gulliver's Travels* by Jonathan Swift)

manhood PHRASE manhood means human nature ❑ *concerning the nature of manhood* (*Gulliver's Travels* by Jonathan Swift)

man-trap NOUN a man-trap is a set of steel jaws that snap shut when trodden on and trap a person's leg

❑ *"Don't go to him," I called out of the window, "he's an assassin! A man-trap!"* (*Oliver Twist* by Charles Dickens)

maps NOUN charts of the night sky ❑ *Let maps to others, worlds on worlds have shown* (*The Good-Morrow* by John Donne)

mark VERB look at or notice ❑ *Mark but this flea, and mark in this* (*The Flea* by John Donne)

maroons NOUN A maroon is someone who has been left in a place which it is difficult for them to escape from, like a small island ❑ *if schooners, islands, and maroons* (*Treasure Island* by Robert Louis Stevenson)

mast NOUN here mast means the fruit of forest trees ❑ *a quantity of acorns, dates, chestnuts, and other mast* (*Gulliver's Travels* by Jonathan Swift)

mate VERB defeat ❑ *Where Mars did mate the warlike Carthigens* (*Doctor Faustus Chorus* by Christopher Marlowe)

mealy ADJ Mealy when used to describe a face meant pallid, pale or colourless ❑ *I only know two sorts of boys. Mealy boys, and beef-faced boys* (*Oliver Twist* by Charles Dickens)

middling ADV fairly or moderately ❑ *she worked me middling hard for about an hour* (*The Adventures of Huckleberry Finn* by Mark Twain)

mill NOUN a mill, or treadmill, was a device for hard labour or punishment in prison ❑ *Was you never on the mill?* (*Oliver Twist* by Charles Dickens)

milliner's shop NOUN a milliner's sold fabrics, clothing, lace and accessories; as time went on they specialized more and more in hats ❑ *to pay their duty to their aunt and to a milliner's shop just over the way* (*Pride and Prejudice* by Jane Austen)

minching un' munching PHRASE how people in the north of England used to describe the way people from the south speak ❑ *Minching un' munching!* (*Wuthering Heights* by Emily Brontë)

mine NOUN gold ❑ *Whether both th'Indias of spice and mine* (*The Sun Rising* by John Donne)

mire NOUN mud ❑ *Tis my fate to be always ground into the mire under the iron heel of oppression* (*The Adventures of Huckleberry Finn* by Mark Twain)

miscellany NOUN a miscellany is a collection of many different kinds of things ❑ *under that, the miscellany began* (*Treasure Island* by Robert Louis Stevenson)

mistarshers NOUN mistarshers means moustache, which is the hair that grows on a man's upper lip ❑ *when he put his hand up to his mistarshers* (*Tess of the D'Urbervilles* by Thomas Hardy)

morrow NOUN here good-morrow means tomorrow and a new and better life ❑ *And now good-morrow to our waking souls* (*The Good-Morrow* by John Donne)

mortification NOUN mortification is an old word for gangrene which is when part of the body decays or "dies" because of disease ❑ *Yes, it was a mortification–that was it* (*The Adventures of Huckleberry Finn* by Mark Twain)

mought VERB mought is an old spelling of might ❑ *what you mought call me? You mought call me captain* (*Treasure Island* by Robert Louis Stevenson)

move VERB move me not means do not make me angry ❑ *Move me not, Faustus* (*Doctor Faustus 2.1* by Christopher Marlowe)

muffin-cap NOUN a muffin-cap is a flat cap made from wool ❑ *the old one, remained stationary in the muffin-cap and leathers* (*Oliver Twist* by Charles Dickens)

mulatter NOUN a mulatter was another word for mulatto, which is a person with parents who are from different races ❑ *a mulatter, most as white as a white man* (*The Adventures of Huckleberry Finn* by Mark Twain)

mummery NOUN mummery is an old word that meant meaningless (or pretentious) ceremony ❑ *When they were all gone, and when Trabb and his men–but not his boy. I looked for him–had crammed their mummery into bags, and were gone too, the house felt wholesomer.* (*Great Expectations* by Charles Dickens)

nap NOUN the nap is the woolly surface on a new item of clothing. Here the surface has been worn away so it looks bare ❑ *like an old hat with the nap rubbed off* (*The Adventures of Huckleberry Finn* by Mark Twain)

natural ■ NOUN a natural is a person born with learning difficulties ❑ *though he had been left to his particular care by their deceased father, who thought him almost a natural.* (*David Copperfield* by Charles Dickens) ■ ADJ natural meant illegitimate ❑ *Harriet Smith was the natural daughter of somebody* (*Emma* by Jane Austen)

navigator NOUN a navigator was originally someone employed to dig canals. It is the origin of the word "navvy" meaning a labourer ❑ *She ascertained from me in a few words what it was all about, comforted Dora, and gradually convinced her that I was not a labourer–from my manner of stating the case I believe Dora concluded that I was a navigator, and went balancing myself up and down a plank all day with a wheelbarrow–and so brought us together in peace.* (*David Copperfield* by Charles Dickens)

necromancy NOUN necromancy means a kind of magic where the magician speaks to spirits or ghosts to find out what will happen in the future ❑ *He surfeits upon cursed necromancy* (*Doctor Faustus chorus* by Christopher Marlowe)

negus NOUN a negus is a hot drink made from sweetened wine and water ❑ *He sat placidly perusing the newspaper, with his little head on one side, and a glass of warm sherry negus at his elbow.* (*David Copperfield* by Charles Dickens)

nice ADJ discriminating. Able to make good judgements or choices ❑ *consequently a claim to be nice* (*Emma* by Jane Austen)

nigh ADV nigh means near ❑ *He'll never know how nigh he come to getting lynched* (*The Adventures of Huckleberry Finn* by Mark Twain)

nimbleness NOUN nimbleness means being able to move very quickly or skilfully ❑ *and with incredible accuracy and nimbleness* (*Treasure Island* by Robert Louis Stevenson)

noggin NOUN a noggin is a small mug or a wooden cup ❑ *you'll bring me one noggin of rum* (*Treasure Island* by Robert Louis Stevenson)

none ADJ neither ❑ *none can die* (*The Good-Morrow* by John Donne)

notices NOUN observations ❑ *Arch are his notices* (*The Prelude* by William Wordsworth)

occiput NOUN occiput means the back of the head ❑ *saw off the occiput of each couple* (*Gulliver's Travels* by Jonathan Swift)

officiously ADV kindly ❑ *the governess who attended Glumdalclitch very officiously lifted me up* (*Gulliver's Travels* by Jonathan Swift)

old salt PHRASE old salt is a slang term for an experienced sailor ❑ *a "true sea-dog", and a "real old salt"* (*Treasure Island* by Robert Louis Stevenson)

or ere PHRASE before ❑ *or ere the Hall was built* (*The Prelude* by William Wordsworth)

ostler NOUN one who looks after horses at an inn ❑ *The bill paid, and the waiter remembered, and the ostler not forgotten, and the chambermaid taken into consideration* (*Great Expectations* by Charles Dickens)

ostry NOUN an ostry is an old word for a pub or hotel ❑ *lest I send you into the ostry with a vengeance* (*Doctor Faustus 2.2* by Christopher Marlowe)

outrunning the constable PHRASE outrunning the constable meant spending more than you earn ❑ *but I shall by this means be able to check your bills and to pull you up if I find you outrunning the constable.* (*Great Expectations* by Charles Dickens)

over ADV across ❑ *It is in length six yards, and in the thickest part at least three yards over* (*Gulliver's Travels* by Jonathan Swift)

over the broomstick PHRASE this is a phrase meaning "getting married without a formal ceremony" ❑ *They both led tramping lives, and this woman in Gerrard-street here, had been married very young, over the broomstick (as we say), to a tramping man, and was a perfect fury in point of jealousy.* (*Great Expectations* by Charles Dickens)

own VERB own means to admit or to acknowledge ❑ *It's my old girl that advises. She has the head. But I never own to it before her. Discipline must be maintained* (*Bleak House* by Charles Dickens)

page NOUN here page means a boy employed to run errands ❑ *not my feigned page* (*On His Mistress* by John Donne)

paid pretty dear PHRASE paid pretty dear means paid a high price or suffered quite a lot ❑ *I paid pretty dear for my monthly fourpenny piece* (*Treasure Island* by Robert Louis Stevenson)

pannikins NOUN pannikins were small tin cups ❑ *of lifting light glasses and cups to his lips, as if they were clumsy pannikins* (*Great Expectations* by Charles Dickens)

pards NOUN pards are leopards ❑ *Not charioted by Bacchus and his pards* (*Ode on a Nightingale* by John Keats)

parlour boarder NOUN a pupil who lived with the family ❑ *and somebody had lately raised her from the condition of scholar to parlour boarder* (*Emma* by Jane Austen)

particular, a London PHRASE London in Victorian times and up to the 1950s was famous for having very dense fog–which was a combination of real fog and the smog of pollution from factories ❑ *This is a London particular . . . A fog, miss* (*Bleak House* by Charles Dickens)

patten NOUN pattens were wooden soles which were fixed to shoes by straps to protect the shoes in wet weather ❑ *carrying a basket like the Great Seal of England in plaited straw, a pair of pattens, a spare shawl, and an umbrella, though it was a fine bright day* (*Great Expectations* by Charles Dickens)

paviour NOUN a paviour was a labourer who worked on the street pavement ❑ *the paviour his pickaxe* (*Oliver Twist* by Charles Dickens)

peccant ADJ peccant means unhealthy ❑ *other peccant humours* (*Gulliver's Travels* by Jonathan Swift)

penetralium NOUN penetralium is a word used to describe the inner rooms of the house ❑ *and I had no desire to aggravate his impatience previous to inspecting the penetralium* (*Wuthering Heights* by Emily Brontë)

pensive ADV pensive means deep in thought or thinking seriously about something ❑ *and she was leaning pensive on a tomb-stone on her right elbow* (*The Adventures of Huckleberry Finn* by Mark Twain)

penury NOUN penury is the state of being extremely poor ❑ *Distress, if not penury, loomed in the distance* (*Tess of the D'Urbervilles* by Thomas Hardy)

perspective NOUN telescope ❑ *a pocket perspective* (*Gulliver's Travels* by Jonathan Swift)

phaeton NOUN a phaeton was an open carriage for four people ❑ *often* *condescends to drive by my humble abode in her little phaeton and ponies* (*Pride and Prejudice* by Jane Austen)

phantasm NOUN a phantasm is an illusion, something that is not real. It is sometimes used to mean ghost ❑ *Experience had bred no fancies in him that could raise the phantasm of appetite* (*Silas Marner* by George Eliot)

physic NOUN here physic means medicine ❑ *there I studied physic two years and seven months* (*Gulliver's Travels* by Jonathan Swift)

pinioned VERB to pinion is to hold both arms so that a person cannot move them ❑ *But the relentless Ghost pinioned him in both his arms, and forced him to observe what happened next.* (*A Christmas Carol* by Charles Dickens)

piquet NOUN piquet was a popular card game in the C18th ❑ *Mr Hurst and Mr Bingley were at piquet* (*Pride and Prejudice* by Jane Austen)

plaister NOUN a plaister is a piece of cloth on which an apothecary (or pharmacist) would spread ointment. The cloth is then applied to wounds or bruises to treat them ❑ *Then, she gave the knife a final smart wipe on the edge of the plaister, and then sawed a very thick round off the loaf: which she finally, before separating from the loaf, hewed into two halves, of which Joe got one, and I the other.* (*Great Expectations* by Charles Dickens)

plantations NOUN here plantations means colonies, which are countries controlled by a more powerful country ❑ *besides our plantations in America* (*Gulliver's Travels* by Jonathan Swift)

plastic ADJ here plastic is an old term meaning shaping or a power that was forming ❑ *A plastic power abode with me* (*The Prelude* by William Wordsworth)

players NOUN actors ❑ *of players which upon the world's stage be* (*On His Mistress* by John Donne)

plump ADV all at once, suddenly ❑ *But it took a bit of time to get it well round, the change come so uncommon plump, didn't it?* (*Great Expectations* by Charles Dickens)

plundered VERB to plunder is to rob or steal from ❑ *These crosses stand for the names of ships or towns that they sank or plundered* (*Treasure Island* by Robert Louis Stevenson)

pommel ■ VERB to pommel someone is to hit them repeatedly with your fists ❑ *hug him round the neck, pommel his back, and kick his legs in irrepressible affection!* (*A Christmas Carol* by Charles Dickens) ■ NOUN a pommel is the part of a saddle that rises up at the front ❑ *He had his gun across his pommel* (*The Adventures of Huckleberry Finn* by Mark Twain)

poor's rates NOUN poor's rates were property taxes which were used to support the poor ❑ *"Oh!" replied the undertaker; "why, you know, Mr. Bumble, I pay a good deal towards the poor's rates."* (*Oliver Twist* by Charles Dickens)

popular ADJ popular means ruled by the people, or Republican, rather than ruled by a monarch ❑ *With those of Greece compared and popular Rome* (*The Prelude* by William Wordsworth)

porringer NOUN a porringer is a small bowl ❑ *Of this festive composition each boy had one porringer, and no more* (*Oliver Twist* by Charles Dickens)

postboy NOUN a postboy was the driver of a horse-drawn carriage ❑ *He spoke to a postboy who was dozing under the gateway* (*Oliver Twist* by Charles Dickens)

post-chaise NOUN a fast carriage for two or four passengers ❑ *Looking round, he saw that it was a post-chaise, driven at great speed* (*Oliver Twist* by Charles Dickens)

postern NOUN a small gate usually at the back of a building ❑ *The little servant happening to be entering the* *fortress with two hot rolls, I passed through the postern and crossed the drawbridge, in her company* (*Great Expectations* by Charles Dickens)

pottle NOUN a pottle was a small basket ❑ *He had a paper-bag under each arm and a pottle of strawberries in one hand . . .* (*Great Expectations* by Charles Dickens)

pounce NOUN pounce is a fine powder used to prevent ink spreading on untreated paper ❑ *in that grim atmosphere of pounce and parchment, red-tape, dusty wafers, ink-jars, brief and draft paper, law reports, writs, declarations, and bills of costs* (*David Copperfield* by Charles Dickens)

pox NOUN pox means sexually transmitted diseases like syphilis ❑ *how the pox in all its consequences and denominations* (*Gulliver's Travels* by Jonathan Swift)

prelibation NOUN prelibation means a foretaste of or an example of something to come ❑ *A prelibation to the mower's scythe* (*The Prelude* by William Wordsworth)

prentice NOUN an apprentice ❑ *and Joe, sitting on an old gun, had told me that when I was 'prentice to him regularly bound, we would have such Larks there!* (*Great Expectations* by Charles Dickens)

presently ADV immediately ❑ *I presently knew what they meant* (*Gulliver's Travels* by Jonathan Swift)

pumpion NOUN pumpkin ❑ *for it was almost as large as a small pumpion* (*Gulliver's Travels* by Jonathan Swift)

punctual ADJ kept in one place ❑ *was not a punctual presence, but a spirit* (*The Prelude* by William Wordsworth)

quadrille ■ NOUN a quadrille is a dance invented in France which is usually performed by four couples ❑ *However, Mr Swiveller had Miss Sophy's hand for the first quadrille (country-dances being low, were utterly proscribed)* (*The Old Curiosity Shop* by Charles Dickens) ■ NOUN quadrille was a card game for four people ❑ *to make up her pool of quadrille in the evening* (*Pride and Prejudice* by Jane Austen)

quality NOUN gentry or upper-class people ❑ *if you are with the quality* (*The Adventures of Huckleberry Finn* by Mark Twain)

quick parts PHRASE quick-witted ❑ *Mr Bennet was so odd a mixture of quick parts* (*Pride and Prejudice* by Jane Austen)

quid NOUN a quid is something chewed or kept in the mouth, like a piece of tobacco ❑ *rolling his quid* (*Treasure Island* by Robert Louis Stevenson)

quit VERB quit means to avenge or to make even ❑ *But Faustus's death shall quit my infamy* (*Doctor Faustus 4.3* by Christopher Marlowe)

rags NOUN divisions ❑ *Nor hours, days, months, which are the rags of time* (*The Sun Rising* by John Donne)

raiment NOUN raiment means clothing ❑ *the mountain shook off turf and flower, had only heath for raiment and crag for gem* (*Jane Eyre* by Charlotte Brontë)

rain cats and dogs PHRASE an expression meaning rain heavily. The origin of the expression is unclear ❑ *But it'll perhaps rain cats and dogs to-morrow* (*Silas Marner* by George Eliot)

raised Cain PHRASE raised Cain means caused a lot of trouble. Cain is a character in the Bible who killed his brother Abel ❑ *and every time he got drunk he raised Cain around town* (*The Adventures of Huckleberry Finn* by Mark Twain)

rambling ADJ rambling means confused and not very clear ❑ *my head began to be filled very early with rambling thoughts* (*Robinson Crusoe* by Daniel Defoe)

raree-show NOUN a raree-show is an old term for a peep-show or a fair-ground entertainment ❑ *A raree-show is here, with children gathered round* (*The Prelude* by William Wordsworth)

recusants NOUN people who resisted authority ❑ *hardy recusants* (*The Prelude* by William Wordsworth)

redounding VERB eddying. An eddy is a movement in water or air which goes round and round instead of flowing in one direction ❑ *mists and steam-like fogs redounding everywhere* (*The Prelude* by William Wordsworth)

redundant ADJ here redundant means overflowing but Wordsworth also uses it to mean excessively large or too big ❑ *A tempest, a redundant energy* (*The Prelude* by William Wordsworth)

reflex NOUN reflex is a shortened version of reflexion, which is an alternative spelling of reflection ❑ *To cut across the reflex of a star* (*The Prelude* by William Wordsworth)

Reformatory NOUN a prison for young offenders/criminals ❑ *Even when I was taken to have a new suit of clothes, the tailor had orders to make them like a kind of Reformatory, and on no account to let me have the free use of my limbs.* (*Great Expectations* by Charles Dickens)

remorse NOUN pity or compassion ❑ *by that remorse* (*On His Mistress* by John Donne)

render VERB in this context render means give. ❑ *and Sarah could render no reason that would be sanctioned by the feeling of the community.* (*Silas Marner* by George Eliot)

repeater NOUN a repeater was a watch that chimed the last hour when a button was pressed–as a result it was useful in the dark ❑ *And his watch is a gold repeater, and worth a hundred pound if it's worth a penny.* (*Great Expectations* by Charles Dickens)

repugnance NOUN repugnance means a strong dislike of something or someone ❑ *overcoming a strong repugnance* (*Treasure Island* by Robert Louis Stevenson)

reverence NOUN reverence means bow. When you bow to someone, you briefly bend your body towards them as a formal way of showing them respect ❑ *made my reverence* (*Gulliver's Travels* by Jonathan Swift)

reverie NOUN a reverie is a daydream ❑ *I can guess the subject of your reverie* (*Pride and Prejudice* by Jane Austen)

revival NOUN a religious meeting held in public ❑ *well I'd ben a-running' a little temperance revival thar' bout a week* (*The Adventures of Huckleberry Finn* by Mark Twain)

revolt VERB revolt means turn back or stop your present course of action and go back to what you were doing before ❑ *Revolt, or I'll in piecemeal tear thy flesh* (*Doctor Faustus 5.1* by Christopher Marlowe)

rheumatics/rheumatism NOUN rheumatics [rheumatism] is an illness that makes your joints or muscles stiff and painful ❑ *a new cure for the rheumatics* (*Treasure Island* by Robert Louis Stevenson)

riddance NOUN riddance is usually used in the form good riddance which you say when you are pleased that something has gone or been left behind ❑ *I'd better go into the house, and die and be a riddance* (*David Copperfield* by Charles Dickens)

rimy ADJ rimy is an adjective which means covered in ice or frost ❑ *It was a rimy morning, and very damp* (*Great Expectations* by Charles Dickens)

riper ADJ riper means more mature or older ❑ *At riper years to Wittenberg he went* (*Doctor Faustus chorus* by Christopher Marlowe)

rubber NOUN a set of games in whist or backgammon ❑ *her father was sure of his rubber* (*Emma* by Jane Austen)

ruffian NOUN a ruffian is a person who behaves violently ❑ *and when the ruffian had told him* (*Treasure Island* by Robert Louis Stevenson)

sadness NOUN sadness is an old term meaning seriousness ❑ *But I prithee tell me, in good sadness* (*Doctor Faustus 2.2* by Christopher Marlowe)

sailed before the mast PHRASE this phrase meant someone who did not look like a sailor ❑ *he had none of the appearance of a man that sailed before the mast* (*Treasure Island* by Robert Louis Stevenson)

scabbard NOUN a scabbard is the covering for a sword or dagger ❑ *Girded round its middle was an antique scabbard; but no sword was in it, and the ancient sheath was eaten up with rust* (*A Christmas Carol* by Charles Dickens)

schooners NOUN A schooner is a fast, medium-sized sailing ship ❑ *if schooners, islands, and maroons* (*Treasure Island* by Robert Louis Stevenson)

science NOUN learning or knowledge ❑ *Even Science, too, at hand* (*The Prelude* by William Wordsworth)

scrouge VERB to scrouge means to squeeze or to crowd ❑ *to scrouge in and get a sight* (*The Adventures of Huckleberry Finn* by Mark Twain)

scrutore NOUN a scrutore, or escritoire, was a writing table ❑ *set me gently on my feet upon the scrutore* (*Gulliver's Travels* by Jonathan Swift)

scutcheon/escutcheon NOUN an escutcheon is a shield with a coat of arms, or the symbols of a family name, engraved on it ❑ *On the scutcheon we'll have a bend* (*The Adventures of Huckleberry Finn* by Mark Twain)

sea-dog PHRASE sea-dog is a slang term for an experienced sailor or pirate ❑ *a "true sea-dog", and a "real old salt,"* (*Treasure Island* by Robert Louis Stevenson)

see the lions PHRASE to see the lions was to go and see the sights of London. Originally the phrase referred to the menagerie in the Tower of London and later in Regent's Park ❑ *We will go and see the lions for an hour or two–it's something to have a fresh fellow like you to show them to, Copperfield* (*David Copperfield* by Charles Dickens)

self-conceit NOUN self-conceit is an old term which means having too high an opinion of oneself, or deceiving yourself ❑ *Till swollen with cunning, of a self-conceit* (*Doctor Faustus chorus* by Christopher Marlowe)

seneschal NOUN a steward ❑ *where a grey-headed seneschal sings a funny chorus with a funnier body of vassals* (*Oliver Twist* by Charles Dickens)

sensible ADJ if you were sensible of something you are aware or conscious of something ❑ *If my children are silly I must hope to be always sensible of it* (*Pride and Prejudice* by Jane Austen)

sessions NOUN court cases were heard at specific times of the year called sessions ❑ *He lay in prison very ill, during the whole interval between his committal for trial, and the coming round of the Sessions.* (*Great Expectations* by Charles Dickens)

shabby ADJ shabby places look old and in bad condition ❑ *a little bit of a shabby village named Pikesville* (*The Adventures of Huckleberry Finn* by Mark Twain)

shay-cart NOUN a shay-cart was a small cart drawn by one horse ❑ *"I were at the Bargemen t'other night, Pip;" whenever he subsided into affection, he called me Pip, and whenever he relapsed into politeness he called me Sir; "when there come up in his* *shay-cart Pumblechook."* (*Great Expectations* by Charles Dickens)

shilling NOUN a shilling is an old unit of currency. There were twenty shillings in every British pound ❑ *"Ten shillings too much," said the gentleman in the white waistcoat.* (*Oliver Twist* by Charles Dickens)

shines NOUN tricks or games ❑ *well, it would make a cow laugh to see the shines that old idiot cut* (*The Adventures of Huckleberry Finn* by Mark Twain)

shirking VERB shirking means not doing what you are meant to be doing, or evading your duties ❑ *some of you shirking lubbers* (*Treasure Island* by Robert Louis Stevenson)

shiver my timbers PHRASE shiver my timbers is an expression which was used by sailors and pirates to express surprise ❑ *why, shiver my timbers, if I hadn't forgotten my score!* (*Treasure Island* by Robert Louis Stevenson)

shoe-roses NOUN shoe-roses were roses made from ribbons which were stuck on to shoes as decoration ❑ *the very shoe-roses for Netherfield were got by proxy* (*Pride and Prejudice* by Jane Austen)

singular ADJ singular means very great and remarkable or strange ❑ *"Singular dream," he says* (*The Adventures of Huckleberry Finn* by Mark Twain)

sire NOUN sire is an old word which means lord or master or elder ❑ *She also defied her sire* (*Little Women* by Louisa May Alcott)

sixpence NOUN a sixpence was half of a shilling ❑ *if she had only a shilling in the world, she would be very lilkely to give away sixpence of it* (*Emma* by Jane Austen)

slavey NOUN the word slavey was used when there was only one servant in a house or boarding-house–so she had to perform all the duties of a larger staff ❑ *Two distinct knocks, sir, will produce the slavey at any time* (*The Old Curiosity Shop* by Charles Dickens)

slender ADJ weak ❑ *In slender accents of sweet verse* (*The Prelude* by William Wordsworth)

slop-shops NOUN slop-shops were shops where cheap ready-made clothes were sold. They mainly sold clothes to sailors ❑ *Accordingly, I took the jacket off, that I might learn to do without it; and carrying it under my arm, began a tour of inspection of the various slop-shops.* (*David Copperfield* by Charles Dickens)

sluggard NOUN a lazy person ❑ *"Stand up and repeat "Tis the voice of the sluggard,'" said the Gryphon.* (*Alice's Adventures in Wonderland* by Lewis Carroll)

smallpox NOUN smallpox is a serious infectious disease ❑ *by telling the men we had smallpox aboard* (*The Adventures of Huckleberry Finn* by Mark Twain)

smalls NOUN smalls are short trousers ❑ *It is difficult for a large-headed, small-eyed youth, of lumbering make and heavy countenance, to look dignified under any circumstances; but it is more especially so, when superadded to these personal attractions are a red nose and yellow smalls* (*Oliver Twist* by Charles Dickens)

sneeze-box NOUN a box for snuff was called a sneeze-box because sniffing snuff makes the user sneeze ❑ *To think of Jack Dawkins–lummy Jack –the Dodger–the Artful Dodger–going abroad for a common twopenny-halfpenny sneeze-box!* (*Oliver Twist* by Charles Dickens)

snorted VERB slept ❑ *Or snorted we in the Seven Sleepers' den?* (*The Good-Morrow* by John Donne)

snuff NOUN snuff is tobacco in powder form which is taken by sniffing ❑ *as he thrust his thumb and fore-finger into the proffered snuff-box of the undertaker: which was an ingenious little model of a patent* *coffin.* (*Oliver Twist* by Charles Dickens)

soliloquized VERB to soliloquize is when an actor in a play speaks to himself or herself rather than to another actor ❑ *"A new servitude! There is something in that," I soliloquized (mentally, be it understood; I did not talk aloud)* (*Jane Eyre* by Charlotte Brontë)

sough NOUN a sough is a drain or a ditch ❑ *as you may have noticed the sough that runs from the marshes* (*Wuthering Heights* by Emily Brontë)

spirits NOUN a spirit is the nonphysical part of a person which is believed to remain alive after their death ❑ *that I might raise up spirits when I please* (*Doctor Faustus 1.5* by Christopher Marlowe)

spleen ■ NOUN here spleen means a type of sadness or depression which was thought to only affect the wealthy ❑ *yet here I could plainly discover the true seeds of spleen* (*Gulliver's Travels* by Jonathan Swift) ■ NOUN irritability and low spirits ❑ *Adieu to disappointment and spleen* (*Pride and Prejudice* by Jane Austen)

spondulicks NOUN spondulicks is a slang word which means money ❑ *not for all his spondulicks and as much more on top of it* (*The Adventures of Huckleberry Finn* by Mark Twain)

stalled of VERB to be stalled of something is to be bored with it ❑ *I'm stalled of doing naught* (*Wuthering Heights* by Emily Brontë)

stanchion NOUN a stanchion is a pole or bar that stands upright and is used as a building support ❑ *and slid down a stanchion* (*The Adventures of Huckleberry Finn* by Mark Twain)

stang NOUN stang is another word for pole which was an old measurement ❑ *These fields were intermingled with woods of half a stang* (*Gulliver's Travels* by Jonathan Swift)

starlings NOUN a starling is a wall built around the pillars that support a bridge to protect the pillars ❑ *There were states of the tide when, having been down the river, I could not get back through the eddy-chafed arches and starlings of old London Bridge* (*Great Expectations* by Charles Dickens)

startings NOUN twitching or night-time movements of the body ❑ *with midnight's startings* (*On His Mistress* by John Donne)

stomacher NOUN a panel at the front of a dress ❑ *but send her aunt the pattern of a stomacher* (*Emma* by Jane Austen)

stoop VERB swoop ❑ *Once a kite hovering over the garden made a stoop at me* (*Gulliver's Travels* by Jonathan Swift)

succedaneum NOUN a succedaneum is a substitute ❑ *But as a succedaneum* (*The Prelude* by William Wordsworth)

suet NOUN a hard animal fat used in cooking ❑ *and your jaws are too weak For anything tougher than suet* (*Alice's Adventures in Wonderland* by Lewis Carroll)

sultry ADJ sultry weather is hot and damp. Here sultry means unpleasant or risky ❑ *for it was getting pretty sultry for us* (*The Adventures of Huckleberry Finn* by Mark Twain)

summerset NOUN summerset is an old spelling of somersault. If someone does a somersault, they turn over completely in the air ❑ *I have seen him do the summerset* (*Gulliver's Travels* by Jonathan Swift)

supper NOUN supper was a light meal taken late in the evening. The main meal was dinner which was eaten at four or five in the afternoon ❑ *and the supper table was all set out* (*Emma* by Jane Austen)

surfeits VERB to surfeit in something is to have far too much of it, or to overindulge in it to an unhealthy degree ❑ *He surfeits upon cursed* *necromancy* (*Doctor Faustus chorus* by Christopher Marlowe)

surtout NOUN a surtout is a long close-fitting overcoat ❑ *He wore a long black surtout reaching nearly to his ankles* (*The Old Curiosity Shop* by Charles Dickens)

swath NOUN swath is the width of corn cut by a scythe ❑ *while thy hook Spares the next swath* (*Ode to Autumn* by John Keats)

sylvan ADJ sylvan means belonging to the woods ❑ *Sylvan historian* (*Ode on a Grecian Urn* by John Keats)

taction NOUN taction means touch. This means that the people had to be touched on the mouth or the ears to get their attention ❑ *without being roused by some external taction upon the organs of speech and hearing* (*Gulliver's Travels* by Jonathan Swift)

Tag and Rag and Bobtail PHRASE the riff-raff, or lower classes. Used in an insulting way ❑ *"No," said he; "not till it got about that there was no protection on the premises, and it come to be considered dangerous, with convicts and Tag and Rag and Bobtail going up and down."* (*Great Expectations* by Charles Dickens)

tallow NOUN tallow is hard animal fat that is used to make candles and soap ❑ *and a lot of tallow candles* (*The Adventures of Huckleberry Finn* by Mark Twain)

tan VERB to tan means to beat or whip ❑ *and if I catch you about that school I'll tan you good* (*The Adventures of Huckleberry Finn* by Mark Twain)

tanyard NOUN the tanyard is part of a tannery, which is a place where leather is made from animal skins ❑ *hid in the old tanyard* (*The Adventures of Huckleberry Finn* by Mark Twain)

tarry ADJ tarry means the colour of tar or black ❑ *his tarry pig-tail* (*Treasure Island* by Robert Louis Stevenson)

thereof PHRASE from there ❑ *By all desires which thereof did ensue* (*On His Mistress* by John Donne)

thick with, be PHRASE if you are "thick with someone" you are very close, sharing secrets–it is often used to describe people who are planning something secret ❑ *Hasn't he been thick with Mr Heathcliff lately?* (*Wuthering Heights* by Emily Brontë)

thimble NOUN a thimble is a small cover used to protect the finger while sewing ❑ *The paper had been sealed in several places by a thimble* (*Treasure Island* by Robert Louis Stevenson)

thirtover ADJ thirtover is an old word which means obstinate or that someone is very determined to do want they want and can not be persuaded to do something in another way ❑ *I have been living on in a thirtover, lackadaisical way* (*Tess of the D'Urbervilles* by Thomas Hardy)

timbrel NOUN timbrel is a tambourine ❑ *What pipes and timbrels?* (*Ode on a Grecian Urn* by John Keats)

tin NOUN tin is slang for money/cash ❑ *Then the plain question is, an't it a pity that this state of things should continue, and how much better would it be for the old gentleman to hand over a reasonable amount of tin, and make it all right and comfortable* (*The Old Curiosity Shop* by Charles Dickens)

tincture NOUN a tincture is a medicine made with alcohol and a small amount of a drug ❑ *with ink composed of a cephalic tincture* (*Gulliver's Travels* by Jonathan Swift)

tithe NOUN a tithe is a tax paid to the church ❑ *and held farms which, speaking from a spiritual point of view, paid highly-desirable tithes* (*Silas Marner* by George Eliot)

towardly ADJ a towardly child is dutiful or obedient ❑ *and a towardly child* (*Gulliver's Travels* by Jonathan Swift)

toys NOUN trifles are things which are considered to have little importance, value, or significance ❑ *purchase my life from them bysome bracelets, glass rings, and other toys* (*Gulliver's Travels* by Jonathan Swift)

tract NOUN a tract is a religious pamphlet or leaflet ❑ *and Joe Harper got a hymn-book and a tract* (*The Adventures of Huckleberry Finn* by Mark Twain)

train-oil NOUN train-oil is oil from whale blubber ❑ *The train-oil and gunpowder were shoved out of sight in a minute* (*Wuthering Heights* by Emily Brontë)

tribulation NOUN tribulation means the suffering or difficulty you experience in a particular situation ❑ *Amy was learning this distinction through much tribulation* (*Little Women* by Louisa May Alcott)

trivet NOUN a trivet is a three-legged stand for resting a pot or kettle ❑ *a pocket-knife in his right; and a pewter pot on the trivet* (*Oliver Twist* by Charles Dickens)

trot line NOUN a trot line is a fishing line to which a row of smaller fishing lines are attached ❑ *when he got along I was hard at it taking up a trot line* (*The Adventures of Huckleberry Finn* by Mark Twain)

troth NOUN oath or pledge ❑ *I wonder, by my troth* (*The Good-Morrow* by John Donne)

truckle NOUN a truckle bedstead is a bed that is on wheels and can be slid under another bed to save space ❑ *It rose under my hand, and the door yielded. Looking in, I saw a lighted candle on a table, a bench, and a mattress on a truckle bedstead.* (*Great Expectations* by Charles Dickens)

trump NOUN a trump is a good, reliable person who can be trusted ❑ *This lad Hawkins is a trump, I perceive* (*Treasure Island* by Robert Louis Stevenson)

tucker NOUN a tucker is a frilly lace collar which is worn around the neck ❑ *Whereat Scrooge's niece's sister–the plump one with the lace tucker: not the one with the roses–blushed.* (*A Christmas Carol* by Charles Dickens)

tureen NOUN a large bowl with a lid from which soup or vegetables are served ❑ *Waiting in a hot tureen!* (*Alice's Adventures in Wonderland* by Lewis Carroll)

turnkey NOUN a prison officer; jailer ❑ *As we came out of the prison through the lodge, I found that the great importance of my guardian was appreciated by the turnkeys, no less than by those whom they held in charge.* (*Great Expectations* by Charles Dickens)

turnpike NOUN the upkeep of many roads of the time was paid for by tolls (fees) collected at posts along the road. There was a gate to prevent people travelling further along the road until the toll had been paid. ❑ *Traddles, whom I have taken up by appointment at the turnpike, presents a dazzling combination of cream colour and light blue; and both he and Mr. Dick have a general effect about them of being all gloves.* (*David Copperfield* by Charles Dickens)

twas PHRASE it was ❑ *twas but a dream of thee* (*The Good-Morrow* by John Donne)

tyrannized VERB tyrannized means bullied or forced to do things against their will ❑ *for people would soon cease coming there to be tyrannized over and put down* (*Treasure Island* by Robert Louis Stevenson)

'un NOUN 'un is a slang term for one–usually used to refer to a person ❑ *She's been thinking the old 'un* (*David Copperfield* by Charles Dickens)

undistinguished ADJ undiscriminating or incapable of making a distinction between good and bad things ❑

their undistinguished appetite to devour everything (*Gulliver's Travels* by Jonathan Swift)

use NOUN habit ❑ *Though use make you apt to kill me* (*The Flea* by John Donne)

vacant ADJ vacant usually means empty, but here Wordsworth uses it to mean carefree ❑ *To vacant musing, unreproved neglect* (*The Prelude* by William Wordsworth)

valetudinarian NOUN one too concerned with his or her own health. ❑ *for having been a valetudinarian all his life* (*Emma* by Jane Austen)

vamp VERB vamp means to walk or tramp to somewhere ❑ *Well, vamp on to Marlott, will 'ee* (*Tess of the D'Urbervilles* by Thomas Hardy)

vapours NOUN the vapours is an old term which means unpleasant and strange thoughts, which make the person feel nervous and unhappy ❑ *and my head was full of vapours* (*Robinson Crusoe* by Daniel Defoe)

vegetables NOUN here vegetables means plants ❑ *the other vegetables are in the same proportion* (*Gulliver's Travels* by Jonathan Swift)

venturesome ADJ if you are venturesome you are willing to take risks ❑ *he must be either hopelessly stupid or a venturesome fool* (*Wuthering Heights* by Emily Bronte)

verily ADV verily means really or truly ❑ *though I believe verily* (*Robinson Crusoe* by Daniel Defoe)

vicinage NOUN vicinage is an area or the residents of an area ❑ *and to his thought the whole vicinage was haunted by her.* (*Silas Marner* by George Eliot)

victuals NOUN victuals means food ❑ *grumble a little over the victuals* (*The Adventures of Huckleberry Finn* by Mark Twain)

vintage NOUN vintage in this context means wine ❑ *Oh, for a draught of vintage!* (*Ode on a Nightingale* by John Keats)

virtual ADJ here virtual means powerful or strong ❑ *had virtual faith* (*The Prelude* by William Wordsworth)

vittles NOUN vittles is a slang word which means food ❑ *There never was such a woman for givin' away vittles and drink* (*Little Women* by Louisa May Alcott)

voided straight PHRASE voided straight is an old expression which means emptied immediately ❑ *see the rooms be voided straight* (*Doctor Faustus 4.1* by Christopher Marlowe)

wainscot NOUN wainscot is wood panel lining in a room so wainscoted means a room lined with wooden panels ❑ *in the dark wainscoted parlor* (*Silas Marner* by George Eliot)

walking the plank PHRASE walking the plank was a punishment in which a prisoner would be made to walk along a plank on the side of the ship and fall into the sea, where they would be abandoned ❑ *about hanging, and walking the plank* (*Treasure Island* by Robert Louis Stevenson)

want VERB want means to be lacking or short of ❑ *The next thing wanted was to get the picture framed* (*Emma* by Jane Austen)

wanting ADJ wanting means lacking or missing ❑ *wanting two fingers of the left hand* (*Treasure Island* by Robert Louis Stevenson)

wanting, I was not PHRASE I was not wanting means I did not fail ❑ *I was not wanting to lay a foundation of religious knowledge in his mind* (*Robinson Crusoe* by Daniel Defoe)

ward NOUN a ward is, usually, a child who has been put under the protection of the court or a guardian for his or her protection ❑ *I call the Wards in Jarndcye. They* *are caged up with all the others.* (*Bleak House* by Charles Dickens)

waylay VERB to waylay someone is to lie in wait for them or to intercept them ❑ *I must go up the road and waylay him* (*The Adventures of Huckleberry Finn* by Mark Twain)

weazen NOUN weazen is a slang word for throat. It actually means shrivelled ❑ *You with a uncle too! Why, I knowed you at Gargery's when you was so small a wolf that I could have took your weazen betwixt this finger and thumb and chucked you away dead* (*Great Expectations* by Charles Dickens)

wery ■ ADV very ❑ *Be wery careful o' vidders all your life* (*Pickwick Papers* by Charles Dickens) ■ *See* wibrated

wherry NOUN wherry is a small swift rowing boat for one person ❑ *It was flood tide when Daniel Quilp sat himself down in the wherry to cross to the opposite shore.* (*The Old Curiosity Shop* by Charles Dickens)

whether PREP whether means which of the two in this example ❑ *we came in full view of a great island or continent (for we knew not whether)* (*Gulliver's Travels* by Jonathan Swift)

whetstone NOUN a whetstone is a stone used to sharpen knives and other tools ❑ *I dropped pap's whetstone there too* (*The Adventures of Huckleberry Finn* by Mark Twain)

wibrated VERB in Dickens's use of the English language "w" often replaces "v" when he is reporting speech. So here "wibrated" means "vibrated". In *Pickwick Papers* a judge asks Sam Weller (who constantly confuses the two letters) "Do you spell it with a 'v' or a 'w'?" to which Weller replies "That depends upon the taste and fancy of the speller, my Lord" ❑ *There are strings . . . in the human heart that had better not be wibrated* (*Barnaby Rudge* by Charles Dickens)

wicket NOUN a wicket is a little door in a larger entrance ❑ *Having rested here, for a minute or so, to collect a good burst of sobs and an imposing show of tears and terror, he knocked loudly at the wicket* (*Oliver Twist* by Charles Dickens)

without CONJ without means unless ❑ *You don't know about me, without you have read a book by the name of The Adventures of Tom Sawyer* (*The Adventures of Huckleberry Finn* by Mark Twain)

wittles ■ NOUN wittles is a slang word which means food ❑ *I live on broken wittles–and I sleep on the coals* (*David Copperfield* by Charles Dickens) ■ *See* wibrated

woo VERB courts or forms a proper relationship with ❑ *before it woo* (*The Flea* by John Donne)

words, to have PHRASE if you have words with someone you have a disagreement or an argument ❑ *I do not want to have words with a young thing like you.* (*Black Beauty* by Anna Sewell)

workhouse NOUN workhouses were places where the homeless were given food and a place to live in return for doing very hard work ❑ *And the Union workhouses? demanded Scrooge. Are they still in operation?* (*A Christmas Carol* by Charles Dickens)

yawl NOUN a yawl is a small boat kept on a bigger boat for short trips. Yawl is also the name for a small fishing boat ❑ *She sent out her yawl, and we went aboard* (*The Adventures of Huckleberry Finn* by Mark Twain)

yeomanry NOUN the yeomanry was a collective term for the middle classes involved in agriculture ❑ *The yeomanry are precisely the order of people with whom I feel I can have nothing to do* (*Emma* by Jane Austen)

yonder ADV yonder means over there ❑ *all in the same second we seem to hear low voices in yonder!* (*The Adventures of Huckleberry Finn* by Mark Twain)